The Challenge of a Long Life

by the same author

DEATH AND THE FAMILY

SECRETS IN THE FAMILY

THE CHALLENGE OF A LONG LIFE

Lily Pincus

with a contribution by Aleda Erskine

FABER AND FABER
London • Boston

First published in 1981
by Faber and Faber Limited
3 Queen Square London WC1N 3AU
Filmset by Latimer Trend & Company Ltd Plymouth
Printed in Great Britain by
Redwood Burn Ltd Trowbridge

British Library Cataloguing in Publication Data

Pincus, Lily
The challenge of a long life
1. Old age
I. Title
305.2′6 HQ1061

ISBN 0-571-11775-9

Morituri salutamus

It is too late! Ah, nothing is too late
Till the tired heart shall cease to palpitate.
Cato learned Greek at eighty; Sophocles
Wrote his grand Oedipus and Simonides
Bore off the prize of verse from his compeers
When each had numbered more than four-score years . . .
Chaucer, at Woodstock with the nightingales,
At sixty wrote the Canterbury Tales:
Goethe at Weimar, toiling to the last,
Completed Faust when eighty years were past.
These are indeed exceptions; but they show
How far the gulf-stream of our youth may flow
Into the arctic regions of our lives . . .
For age is opportunity no less
Than youth itself, though in another dress
And as the evening twilight fades away
The sky is filled with stars, invisible by day . . .

LONGFELLOW

Contents

	Foreword	13
1.	Personal experiences of eighty-three years	15
2.	Loss throughout the life-cycle	31
3.	The importance of the family	46
4.	Dependence/independence/interdependence	65
5.	Relationships with contemporaries	78
6.	Physical and mental health in old age	92
7.	The search for a meaning	110
8.	Retirement *by Aleda Erskine*	124
	Bibliography *by Lily Pincus and Aleda Erskine*	151

I am deeply grateful to the numerous friends and colleagues who have contributed to the book by giving me their interest, support and stories. Because the latter have to remain anonymous, I cannot name the contributors and only hope they know that without them the book could not have been written.

I also wish to acknowledge my deep gratitude to colleagues and medical specialists who have given generously of their time for discussions from which I have greatly benefited.

The encouragement, patience and understanding of our editor, Susan Kennedy, as well as her many useful suggestions, have been of immeasurable help to Aleda Erskine and myself throughout the writing of this book.

Foreword

What is it in an individual's life-history that determines his or her experience of old age? Why is it that some people achieve a happy, active or even creative long life, while others merely survive, or withdraw into apathy and confusion? I ask these questions in relation to my own age group, the 'old-old' or over seventy-fives, a group that I feel has been neglected by other writers and relegated by and large to the status of mere hangers-on to life in a perpetually twilit antechamber to death.

I hope that the book will make a contribution to the social challenges posed by the 'greying of the nations' and the changing structure of the family in the western world. It aims to foster and encourage the growing questioning of the stereotypes of old age by many gerontologists and writers, and most importantly by many of the new generation of the over-sixties who are beginning to evolve a life-style which reflects and satisfies their individual needs. This questioning will, I hope, have a liberating effect on the 'old-old', and may help to change the expectations and attitudes of the relatives, friends and professional people who care for them; for as long as society regards old people as helpless and tiresome, they will feel that that is what they are expected to be. Because the attitudes of the 'young-old', those of around retirement age, play such a vital part in helping to create the image the over seventy-fives have of themselves, I invited Aleda Erskine to contribute a final chapter to the book dealing with the whole question of retirement.

The Challenge of a Long Life is not a psychogeriatric treatise, nor a 'Spock' for the elderly, nor does it attempt to grapple with sociological questions. It aims to explore those psychological issues that appear to be most relevant to the quality of a long life, issues illustrated through life-stories which show the strong individuality of old people.

I have chosen this method of conveying my impressions of contemporary old age in western society because I have always found life-stories more convincing than theories. And because this is a very personal book, I am starting it with an account of my own life. In writing it, I had hoped to find some answers to the question of what makes for a good long life, but now I shall be content if it helps others in a further search.

CHAPTER ONE

Personal experiences of eighty-three years

I was born in 1898 in Karlsbad (a famous spa in Bohemia, at that time part of the Austro-Hungarian Empire), as the first and much longed for child of liberal Jewish middle-class parents, who lived within a close network of family relationships. This was broken, or at least considerably loosened, when my father had to move to Berlin for business reasons. I was five years old and my brother Oscar was two, when my family left Karlsbad. A second brother, Max, was born two years later, more or less on doctor's orders, because my mother had developed all sorts of nervous complaints in the unfamiliar surroundings of Berlin. It was hoped that a new baby would help her to overcome her feelings of strangeness. She was a devoted mother and her children were always the centre of her life.

Although the change and my mother's depression cannot have been easy for a five-year-old, I appear to have adjusted quickly. It was probably the support of my affectionate family that helped to keep intact my trust and curiosity about everything new in life. Our flat was on the banks of the Spree, and the excitement of the passing boats seemed to make up for the loss of the beautiful Karlsbad woods. These had been my earlier playground, and I had been inseparable from my playmates there, two girl cousins; I had even insisted on wearing the same clothes as they did. Perhaps it was the experience of this close relationship that helped me to find a new friend—Lotte—quickly in Berlin. She lived in the same house, we started together at the same school, and spent all our spare time with each other. When I asked to wear the same clothes as Lotte it became clear that I had transferred onto her my need for close identification.

At school I was happy from the beginning, made friends easily, but learnt little. My carefree attitude was supported by the head of the school who often said that it was more important to him that his girls should be happy and loveable than that they learnt much. In spite of my laziness there was never any trouble at school. I managed to get along without any ambitions with the minimum of effort. Required to do hardly any homework, I seemed to have put what energy and sensitivity I had into my personal relationships.

The link with Karlsbad was maintained by visits of members of the family, and as soon as Oscar and I were able to travel alone, we spent our summer holidays there with our aunts who always made us warmly welcome. The enjoyable weeks we spent there, resuming contact with our cousins and their friends, preserved the continuity with our early life and memories.

I don't know at what point in my happy life I became aware that my beloved Karlsbad was not only a place for pleasure and enjoyment, but was full of conflicts. The people who came to drink the waters were mostly wealthy foreigners whose life-style was very different from that of the local townspeople. Shops and amenities were geared to their requirements, so that the residents were made to feel like second-class citizens in their own town. In addition to the tensions this caused were those that existed between the German and Czech-speaking citizens of Bohemia. My relatives were all German Jews, with the emphasis on German, and did not want to have anything to do with the Czech population. When my favourite cousin Elsa fell in love with an intelligent and attractive Czech engineer, the family was incensed, demanding that she should give up her association with a member of an inferior race. She fled to my parents who supported her, which made me proud of them and also gave me the opportunity to follow the exciting romance from close at hand. In the end, Elsa's parents gave in. She married her engineer and when, after the 1914–18 war and the collapse of the Austrian Empire, Karlsbad and the Sudetenland became part of the newly created Czechoslovakia, the inferior race became the superior one.

How Elsa's family could have sought to destroy her love for this man was incomprehensible to me. A couple of years earlier their eldest daughter, after marrying a man they highly approved of, had committed suicide on her honeymoon. The cause of this tragedy was never explained; yet I felt that it must have had something to do with the shock of the first sexual experience, although, at twelve years old, I had no idea of what such an experience might be. Now, in my old age, I realize how important it was for my development to experience and accept at an early age the negative aspects of the place and the relatives I loved, and to go on loving them.

The most important part of my life continued to be my friendships which, about this time, widened to include boy-friends. The only serious one, Eric, I had inherited, so to speak, from an older girl on whom I had a crush at school (such infatuations were much encouraged). When this particular girl had proved unfaithful to both of us, Eric and I comforted each other by consuming together masses of cakes and hot chocolate. Eric lived opposite our house on the other side of the Spree. We decided we would feel closer to each other at night if we slept outside on our respective balconies. My father shook his head but nevertheless helped me to carry my mattress onto the balcony and kissed me good-night with a loving 'Sleep well, silly girl.' Fortunately, the nights were warm in the summer of 1914.

In August of that year war broke out. Eric was called up, and disappeared from my life. A couple of months later I left school, and my carefree childhood came to an end. I must have had a dim awareness of this, since I can remember on my last day at school weeping bitterly and trying in vain to cool my tear-stained face under the old-fashioned watertap in the corridor.

During our last months at school, in an atmosphere of patriotic enthusiasm, our teachers had impressed on us the need to choose a training which would benefit Germany's war effort. My friend Lotte had chosen to do a two-year course in scientific photography, including x-ray work. I had no idea what I wanted to do, but as I wished to remain close to Lotte, I elected to study the same course. However, I was aware that, although she was eminently suited for it, I was not. It was therefore a great blow to me when Lotte had to abandon the course after a few months; because her father was of Russian origin, she was considered an enemy alien.

Since I have always been inept in technical matters I found the handling of precious and complicated instruments a great trial, often resulting in disaster. However, the fact that I could relate easily and happily to the patients who came for x-ray treatment helped my teachers to tolerate me, and enabled me to plod on. I did not know until much later that my work with x-rays, at this time carried out without any protection, would result in the greatest tragedy of my life, my inability to have children.

In the spring of 1916 my father, who had been unwell for some time, was found to have cancer of the liver. He was not expected to live long. I decided I wanted to stay at home and help with the nursing, and so gave up the course. I did not feel this to be a sacrifice when measured against the traumatic loss I had now to face, but the remaining months of my father's life were far from unhappy. Cancer of the liver is extremely painful, yet my father never complained and bore his illness with quiet dignity. Knowing that he was dying, he carefully set his affairs in order, but never spoke about it. Only once, when we three children were sitting by his bed, and Max was reading a story to him, did he say with a loving smile: 'It isn't easy to leave such children.'

The greatest part of the nursing was shared between fifteen-year-old Oscar and myself. Our highly strung mother was often unwell, and we felt she had to be spared avoidable suffering. Max was only eleven years old. Yet, when wartime food shortages became severe, he developed a genius for discovering sources of unrationed food. On our father's last day he had been queuing since early in the morning for some eggs. I shall never forget his shocked face when his radiant expression of joy over his achievement was shattered by the news that our father had died during his absence. Oscar had had his Barmizvah two years earlier, and so had to perform after my father's death all the tasks required of a male Jew. He did it all with great self-control, but his falling ill a few weeks later with kidney trouble may have reflected the great strain he was under. He and I were supporting each other at this time and, in spite of our youth, were able to provide some strength for the rest of the family.

My father's peaceful death made a deep impression on me, making me aware of the importance of the atmosphere around a death-bed. That I had been able not to allow my own feelings of loss burden my father's dying became a source of growth and strength to me. From then on, without consciously seeking it, I found myself often at a death-bed. This did not affect my joy of life; it almost strengthened it and helped me to mature. I also began to use my gift for positive personal relationships, previously restricted to my family and friends, in a more conscious way. I started to spend my spare time with deprived Jewish children at a day hostel in the east end of Berlin, and, needing to earn my living, took a job which involved dealing with prisoners of war and their families. This work made the tragedy of war more real to me. It was important because none of my family, nor any of my close friends, had relatives in danger at the front, and I lacked the gift of compassionate identification with what I had not experienced.

As the war went on, news of great losses and the first doubts about the certainty of a German victory, combined with severe shortages of food and fuel, led to a growing depression. In the winter of 1917 this was increased by the outbreak of Spanish 'flu. Many, particularly young people, died in the epidemic. Among them were several of my schoolmates, people I had known well, and this loss of young lives was disturbing in a way that was different from the loss of young lives in battle. Yet I was able to maintain a fundamentally hopeful attitude to life until, quite suddenly, my friend Lotte died, only a few days after undergoing what had seemed to be a harmless operation, apparently the result of neglect in an under-staffed hospital.

Lotte's death, so soon after the losses of the 'flu epidemic, stirred up my uncompleted mourning for my father. For a few months I was very depressed. But then my inherent love of and curiosity about life took over again. I enjoyed my work, where I was popular, and made a special friend of one of my colleagues whose cultured, liberal Jewish family lived near my own home. Our friendship deepened when, in the spring of 1918, her father died quite suddenly. Her brother Fritz, an officer in the German army, came home from the front but was too late for the funeral. This added to his distress. When I met him, our mutual experience of death and loss made an immediate strong bond. Soon afterwards Fritz had to return to the front and the enforced separation seemed to increase our need for each other.

A few months later the war was over and Fritz came home. Germany was defeated after four and a half years of terrible losses. The country, the soldiers, the workers were in rebellion. The Kaiser left for Holland and most of the princes disappeared from their estates—they simply were not needed any more. Political authority was taken over by the Social Democratic party, and in November 1918 the Weimar Republic was proclaimed. Its task was doomed from the beginning, largely through the refusal of the victorious nations to make any concessions in the Versailles peace treaty that might have enabled the democratic elements in Germany to gain support. Instead, the increasing hopelessness of the situation played into the hands of reactionary and belligerent sections of the population.

All my sympathies were with the newly-proclaimed Weimar Republic but I had never been active politically and was looking to my friends for guidance. Most of them were as confused as I was, especially those men who had come back from the war to a humiliated Germany. To them the Weimar Republic represented some hope for a better future. To settle down was especially difficult for those soldiers, like Fritz, whose personal situation had fundamentally changed too. His family, used to great comfort and the help of several servants, was suddenly very poor and not at all equipped to cope with it. Worst of all, it was now impossible for Fritz to continue his law studies as he had immediately to find a way to earn not only his own but, as far as possible, his family's living.

In this atmosphere of struggle, the friendship between us grew. My positive attitude towards new and challenging situations was of some help to Fritz, and his clearer understanding of and more committed involvement in political and social concerns and upheavals helped me not to remain just an interested onlooker. In spite of our increasing participation in such concerns, we found time and energy to enjoy ourselves. The tone for this was set a few days after Fritz's return home. I was invited to a private fancy-dress ball and Fritz came with me. We had great fun at the ball and afterwards continued dancing in the street until dawn.

Although we soon decided to make our life together we did not marry for three years. In spite of the hardships, the confusion, and the insecurity of the post-war period, these were personally good years for us. We married in 1922 and, as we both adored children, we hoped to start a family immediately. When I failed to become pregnant we went from doctor to doctor for help. It was several years before it was discovered that my fertility had been destroyed through my work with x-rays. At the time of my training the destructive powers of these rays were unknown; as a result neither I nor any of my fellow female students were able to conceive. Only later, when sufficient publicity had been gained for x-ray victims who had lost arms or hands, were precautionary measures taken.

To add to our personal problems the confusions of what has become known as the crazy 1920s (which actually lasted until the beginning of the Nazi period) began to make their impact on the post-war generation. There was on the one hand much poverty and unemployment, political upheaval, great uncertainty about the future, and a rapidly growing inflation, in which middle-class families, including Fritz's and my own, lost all the money they had. On the other hand, just at that time Berlin became the cultural centre of Europe with exciting theatres, outstanding political cabarets, and the highest achievements in music and the arts, of which the Bauhaus is the most important example. Night-clubs grew like mushrooms, fancy-dress balls, often several on the same night, expressed people's need to forget reality for a while. Money was spent lavishly. It was anyhow useless the next day. How we managed to find sufficient energy and time to combine pleasurable escapes with our commitment to the struggle against approaching catastrophe is retrospectively incomprehensible to me.

It was an exciting life, but also a very strenuous one, and as Fritz and I had always dreamt of a life in the country, we were delighted when the opportunity arose to get some distance away from the frenetic atmosphere of Berlin. In the spring of 1924 we moved with friends who had two small children into a house with a big garden on an island near Potsdam. There we set up a shared household based on mutual trust and affection without any theories about communal living. This move gave new meaning to my life and helped me to recover from the shattering discovery that I could not have children. The inner and outer situation of the house soon made it a meeting place, and later a refuge, for family and friends, a place which meant much to many people of different backgrounds and interests.

Both husbands continued to work in Berlin, which meant a long and tiring journey but helped us to keep in close contact with the exciting and threatened city during the years of the Weimar Republic and its collapse, coinciding with the rise of the Nazi Party. Friends, whom we chose without prejudice of religion, race, sex or social group, not only enriched our lives but also saw to it that we did not withdraw into a cosy country life, and maintained our involvement with increasingly pressing issues. Especially Fritz's closest friend Saul. Highly intelligent, well informed and politically active, he contributed what he called *idiotenstunden* (lessons for idiots) about national and international developments. These meetings became important regular events for us and our friends, and added to the attraction of the house. I was too shy to speak in these discussions and always hoped that one of my friends would say what I could not find the words for myself. That I can now talk to large groups of people in a language which to some extent has remained a foreign one, and enjoy doing so, still fills me with wonder.

Although Fritz and I were different in temperament we shared many of the same attitudes to life. We were both Socialists, Fritz the better informed and more committed one; we were both brought up without a Jewish tradition and without belonging to a Jewish community. We both had many non-Jewish friends, and neither of us had in the past experienced anti-sematisim. I had only once in my childhood come up against it, when I found my brother Oscar, then eight years old, and his best friend, the son of an aristocratic family, sobbing in each other's arms because the friend's parents had not allowed him to invite a Jew to his birthday party.

After the war, when Oscar left school, his headmaster asked him whether he was upset that Karlsbad and the Sudetenland had become Czech and not, as had been expected, German. Oscar replied that he believed in the League of Nations and was hoping that national boundaries would become increasingly unimportant. His headmaster immediately said that he believed this because he was a Jew and could not identify with German sovereignty. Oscar had planned to study law and become a judge, but after this conversation he felt that he would never be able to represent German law.

Fritz had been an officer in the German Army, and felt himself to be unreservedly German, as did most of our friends. During the 1920s we never considered ourselves to be outsiders; in fact we felt ourselves as important members of that part of the German population which wanted and was working for a democratic Germany. In spite of the many warning signs that showed a development in the opposite direction, we were shocked and surprised when the Nazis came to power on 30 January, 1933.

How unprepared we were may be judged by our going, the night before this unforgettable date, the date which changed our lives and the face of the world, to a fancy-dress ball in the Academy of Arts where many left-wing artists had their studios. Soon after midnight a group of uniformed men appeared, and unaware of what had happened during the last few hours, the dancers at first thought the uniforms were costumes. But the men, the first members of the Gestapo we had encountered, made their real status clear with brutal force, sealed the studios, and drove out the dancers. That was the end of the fancy-dress ball, and of much else.

Although the conservative Potsdam population and the local

police were reluctant followers of the new régime and as protective as possible of the few resident Jewish families, the visits of left-wing guests to our house attracted the interest of the Gestapo. Their searching calls became frequent and after the burning of the Reichstag, friends who had sought shelter in our house were arrested there.

As the persecution of the Jews grew, so did our identification with the persecuted. The house became increasingly the refuge for people who felt threatened in their own homes. Partly because Fritz and I did not look 'Jewish', we could be helpful in many different ways, such as taking people to hiding places; removing dangerous reading matter from their homes; or helping them to get out of the country. I worked at that time at a radiologist's surgery situated in a Berlin corner-house where, with the help of a non-Jewish colleague, I established a soup kitchen for people who neither dared to go out shopping nor to eat in restaurants. Our non-Jewish boss pretended not to notice what was going on.

From 1937 onwards, when a Jewish boarding school in our neighbourhood had to close down, we offered a home to those children, at one time about twenty, whose parents were in concentration camps or had already given up their homes in preparation to emigrate. With all this Fritz and I were so busy and felt so much needed, that we had not considered leaving the country until the '*Kristallnacht*', the pogrom of November 1938, when synagogues were burnt down, Jewish premises destroyed, and innumerable Jews arrested or assaulted. It became clear that for us, too, emigration was the only alternative to concentration camp.

A nice Froebel teacher was prepared to look after those children who had to remain in the house for the time being. All of them reached safety within the next few months. We had no close relatives to consider leaving behind as Fritz's two sisters and my two brothers had already left Germany, and so had the friends with whom we had shared the house. My mother had died in Karlsbad in 1930, surrounded by her three children for whom the shared experience of her peaceful death had become a renewed bond. Fritz's mother, who had come to live with us when she became terminally ill, had died in 1937, a conscious and radiant death in a room filled with flowers for her seventieth birthday. She had always been an anxious, helpless woman, frightened of life, yet her death became an unforgettable experience for all who had the privilege to witness it, and for me a confirmation that death should be seen as a friend rather than an enemy.

After the '*Kristallnacht*' pogrom, the local police had come to arrest my husband, who was working in Berlin. This warning enabled him to go into hiding, where he stayed until our British visas arrived. These had been arranged by an influential British acquaintance of Fritz's sister and her husband, and arrived surprisingly quickly. Not only were we and our German friends greatly relieved, but the Potsdam police as well, when we began to arrange the necessary formalities for emigration, which were completed in February 1939. By that time immigration laws had been tightened, and we were only allowed to take 10 RM each and one small suitcase, which was not to contain any valuables. But losing material possessions did not seem important, although we each mourned one special loss. For Fritz it was his grand piano, as playing it, especially music by Bach, had always been his comfort; and I found it so difficult to leave the garden which I had created and loved that I could never again find pleasure in gardening.

Although the relief of actually getting away from the terrors of the last months (or rather six years) was the most dominant feeling, the actual departure turned out to be a nightmare. A large group of friends had gathered at the airport, many of them disregarding the danger for their own safety. Leaving them, not knowing if we would ever meet again, was most painful, especially leaving Saul, who in spite of offers of several jobs abroad refused to emigrate as he felt he was needed by those Jews who had to stay on in Germany. Our farewell was cut short by an official who took us away for a special investigation, including the physical examination of every opening of our bodies, to make sure that we had not used them to conceal any of our own jewellery or money. For this examination the scheduled flight was delayed by a whole hour.

When at last we sat in our plane we were exhausted, but full of confidence for a new life. That we were greeted in London by Fritz's sister and brother-in-law, who had recently arrived from China, helped to minimize feelings of strangeness. They invited us to stay with them in a boarding house until our guarantor arranged for us to go to a small village in Wales, where he had founded a Working Men's College. He knew that it would be impossible for us to get work permits and that life in London would be difficult and expensive. The college was beautifully situated, overlooking sea and mountains, and the life with the Welsh working men was a new and exciting experience for us. I helped in the kitchen, and Fritz did all sorts of odd jobs, unpaid of course. We had our meals in the college and our guarantor made us an allowance which supplied what little money we needed. We loved the beautiful Welsh countryside and the Welsh people. That we were not burdened with possessions turned out to be a great blessing. We had lived for fifteen years in our island home, where we could offer generous hospitality to many. We had been well-known, both professionally and personally, and had wide contacts. Now all this was lost and we started a new life in a strange land, without any of the things which had provided us with a social and material frame. It was a tremendous challenge, for we now had nothing but our individual personalities with which to make contacts. Fritz was forty-five and I was forty when we began this life, dependent on hospitality and charity, but full of exciting new impressions which stirred our curiosity and imagination.

The outbreak of war in September 1939 brought great anxiety about friends and relatives in Germany and Nazi-occupied countries, but it was also a great relief as it seemed to be the only hope of bringing an end to the Nazi régime. Our own status changed from that of refugees from oppression to that of enemy aliens which meant that our movements were restricted; we had to report to the friendly local police, and after some time Fritz was interned and remained so for nine months. The Welsh miners were called up and the college building was taken over by departments of the University of Liverpool, who offered me a job as an assistant house-mistress with a small salary. After some time I was told that they might not be able to continue my employment because I was an enemy alien. As I now needed some money to send to Fritz, and to my two brothers who had also arrived in Wales and were interned, the loss of my job would have created considerable problems. Fortunately, the staff of the college found a way out of the difficulties and I could stay on.

That our changed status had not affected the trust and affection which was shown to us by the Welsh population and the English wartime visitors was a great comfort. The friendships which started during this difficult time became our greatest gains and contributed much to the fact that we both emerged from all our tribulations with increased inner security and unchanging hopefulness.

When the war was over we became British subjects, were allowed to accept paid non-domestic work, and moved to London. Fritz was employed by the BBC, and I had the good luck to be offered a job as a social worker in a voluntary casework agency. It would never have occurred to me to apply for such a job as I had no academic qualifications, but I very soon knew that I had found my vocation. Five years later I was asked to join a developmental unit in which social work methods and psychotherapy were used for dealing with marital problems. This work, which involved the need to increase self-awareness, has probably become the major factor in shaping my old age.

The positive developments in our personal lives were overshadowed by the devastating news which reached us at the end of the war. The murder of six million Jews, the deaths of relatives and friends, among them Saul, in concentration camps, the extent of the destruction of many parts of Europe, the fact of Hiroshima, all this revealed the ever-growing effects of human aggression and obscured the hope of peace. Fritz was so affected by these worrying developments that he began to show symptoms of illness. On the night of the peace celebration, while we were watching the fireworks from the roof of the BBC building, he suddenly fainted and had to be taken to hospital. Soon after that night it became clear that he was really ill, but only in 1952, at the first of many operations, was cancer diagnosed. We shared the knowledge of his terminal illness from the beginning. Fritz continued to live for eleven years, full of interest in life and the world, full of love and affection and often fun. He died at home in May 1963 a triumphant death, having remained conscious to the last hour.

During the long years of Fritz's illness it was difficult to combine the care for him with my work, which was making increasing demands on me but also offered increasing gratification. Fritz shared my experiences with great interest but especially in his last years he was most concerned that his illness should not disrupt my career too much, as he rightly foresaw that this would be my greatest support when he had to leave me. After his death I worked doubly hard, partly because it filled a need of mine but partly to justify his concern which had often deprived him of my company. I felt I had to prove to him that his sacrifice had been worthwhile and in doing so I derived still deeper satisfaction from my work which I continued until I was seventy-five years old. Then I felt it was time to retire from employment, but although I had already established a small private psychotherapeutic practice I found the decision to leave my work unit and my colleagues very difficult. I cheered up when, a few days after I had posted my letter of resignation, an American publisher asked me to write for him. This surprising development was the beginning of my new career. Although in the context of my work I had contributed to and edited various publications, and had much enjoyed doing so, I had never thought of myself as an author. The first book I wrote, out of a deep need of mine and without literary ambitions, was about death and bereavement. It was published at a time when the death taboo was just beginning to lift and appeared to meet the need of many people from all over the world. Encouraged by this response I continued to write about those human problems which I had encountered in my work. With each book I learned a little more about myself.*

* *Death and the Family*, Faber & Faber, 1976; *Secrets in the Family*, Faber & Faber, 1978.

Now, at eighty-two, I live alone in the flat in which Fritz died, in a house with congenial and supportive neighbours and a view over wide green fields. A friendly helpful woman, herself in her seventies, comes three times each week for an hour or two to tidy up my flat and do my washing. There are many things which neither she nor I are able to do, such as standing on steps, or anything that requires a strong grip. She has been with me for over twenty years; I value her support and we care for each other.

In spite of all these positives in my surroundings, it is by no means always easy to live alone, partly because I am singularly stupid about all technical problems. Physically I am quite well except for some rheumatism and increasing unreliability of digestive functions. I can see and hear, not as well as in the past, but well enough not to be bothered. My only trouble is that I am rather wobbly on my legs and have to be careful not to fall, using a stick when in doubt. Not long ago, on a cold winter morning, I was unable to shut a window from inside and when I stepped in my nightie onto the balcony to try from outside, I fell and could not get up again. It was bitterly cold and I felt helpless. Just then I remembered a television programme in which the actress Edith Evans, in her eighties, was interviewed. To the question what did she find most difficult in old age, she said: 'Falling,' and turning to the audience she went on: 'You will fall, you can't help it but if you do, don't try to get up, stay where you are.' In my position I found this advice so funny that I had to laugh and suddenly found the strength to wriggle myself back into the room.

I have always loved my sleep and on the whole I am a good sleeper; now I find it difficult not to nod off whenever I sit down. It is very tempting to succumb to this but I know how dangerous it is as it can easily stop active living, one of the main requirements for a good long life. Except for this battle not to fall asleep too often, I take my various old-age failures, such as losing things, dropping, spilling, forgetting, not too seriously. I agree with Professor Richard Doll, himself approaching seventy, who says: 'People over sixty-five should be prepared to accept death but live to the full and enjoy life rather than to try to live a little longer. It is a responsibility of the old to live dangerously rather than expect the Health Service to spend a lot of money to keep them alive longer.'*

I am not afraid to ask for help if I need it. The other day I had quite a long walk to do and a heavy bag to carry, when suddenly I could not go on. There was no bench in sight, no place to rest, and the only person passing by was a school-boy of about twelve years. When he was near enough I asked whether he would do his good deed for the day and carry my bag. He took it rather grumpily, then, after a few steps, offered me his arm and a few steps further demanded: 'Stand still and breathe.' I did this obediently, which seemed to please him, for he repeated his command after every few steps and when I let him know that I had recovered my strength and spirit, he insisted on taking me all the way to my destination. On this, as on similar occasions, I feel that such help from the young to the old is mutually beneficial.

I am happy to have friends of all ages, as I feel that living mainly among contemporaries can encourage a pre-occupation with old-age problems and result in the sort of segregation that narrows the view of life. I hope to continue to live in mutually helpful relationships with young and old people, and to contribute a little to diminish for both the often irrational fear of old age and the aged.

* Quoted by Morton Puner, *To the Good Long Life*, Universe Books, 1975, p. 31.

CHAPTER TWO

Loss throughout the life-cycle

Now let us look at another life-story, one from a very different background from my own, that has been full of losses. Beatrice is seventy-five years old and has been widowed for eighteen years. She supplements her old-age pension by going out to char three mornings each week for a couple of employers for whom she has worked for several decades. Although she now gets easily tired and there are many things which she can no longer do, she is greatly valued by them, and they think of her as a friend. Much of her free time she uses to look after an ailing brother and sister, the only surviving of her nine siblings. And she spends much of her time with the children of a younger brother who died a year ago. Her main concern is always to do something for people who need her. She never had children of her own, and is anxious not to make demands on her various nephews and nieces, although she knows how fond they are of her and how much they want to give her help and some pleasure, for which she has a great capacity of enjoyment.

Listening to her life-story, one wonders how she acquired her warmth, contentment and ability to love. She was the youngest but one in the family, with one brother born eighteen months after her. Her father worked on the railway, and drank or gambled most of his money away, so that the mother had to go out to work as a school-cleaner. This meant getting up at 5 o'clock each morning and working hard at scrubbing stone floors. She began to get ill with cancer when Beatrice was five, and died when she was seven. The father wanted to put the five school-age children into a home but the eldest daughter refused to let this happen and took over the care of her younger brothers and sisters. They were desperately poor and on pay day often went to the railway to get some money from the father before he wasted it. Yet one of

Beatrice's favourite stories is about a blind neighbour who used to say how lucky she was to live next door to these children whose laughter kept her alive.

Beatrice left school at fourteen, went to work in a factory and there fell in love with a boy aged fifteen. They courted for twelve years, then married, and went to live in his family's house. Her husband was delicate, suffering from bronchial asthma. He could at best do light work, but much of the time no work at all. His father, who continued to live with the couple, was also an invalid, and for most of her married life Beatrice took charring jobs, and got up very early to look after the two men and the home before going out to work. She never complained, and managed to maintain her cheerfulness and sense of humour.

When her husband and her father-in-law died within a few months of each other, her husband's brother inherited the house in which she had lived all her married life. He sold it and she had to leave, but was offered two rooms by another relative in a house that was due to be demolished. When this happened Beatrice was lucky to get a modern council flat of which she is the very proud and hospitable owner. Poor, old or sick relatives, friends and neighbours are always made welcome, even if they only come for a cup of tea and a nap by the fire. Although she has never stopped missing her husband, and gets upset about her many physical handicaps, her main concern is not to let anybody down who may need her help. She manages well on her limited income, is always ready to count her blessings, and gets angry when other old people complain about their situation.

To understand why a good, happy and fulfilled old age is achieved by some, and not by others, old age must be seen, not in isolation or in generalized terms, but as a part of the individual life-cycle. I hope that Beatrice's life story, like my own, will have helped to illuminate for the reader my belief that the way we cope with loss and separation is the basis for the development of our personality, determining our process of growth from the moment of leaving the womb to the last breath we draw.

Living involves constant changes, and each change, each giving up of a familiar situation for an unknown new one, can lead to a crisis. Not only serious illness, physical deterioration, the loss of a limb, of sight or hearing, a change of job, retirement or moving home, but also such events as marriage, the birth of children, children leaving home, significant separations and most especially death and bereavement, can constitute crises of loss. Eric Ericson speaks of crises as 'turning points, which are parts of the life of every individual and of every family, crucial periods of increased vulnerability and heightened potential.'* Each crisis of loss that can be overcome will help towards the overcoming of future ones; the giving up of the familiar need not be experienced merely as a loss but, through the acceptance of the new situation, as a challenge, with the potential for growth.

This process of development begins with birth, when the baby loses the stillness, the warmth, the safety of the womb. What this first crisis means is shown vividly by pictures of screaming, frantic new-born babies which contrast so dramatically with those of the proud, joyfully beaming parents and the highly satisfied midwives and doctors. Dr Frederic Leboyer has shown in his film and book *Birth without Violence* that being born need not be such a terrifying experience. It is his firmly-held conviction that if this first crisis, this first step into the unknown, can be made a quiet, peaceful and comfortable experience, then the new being is more likely to start on his or her life's journey full of trust. He will not only have a better chance of overcoming later inevitable crises but, thanks to his readiness to accept change trustfully, will find in them new satisfaction and gain, compensating for the loss.

Even at this very first moment, it is not possible to speak of the baby in isolation, but always of the mother and the baby, and in all the various phases of development, in all the manifold crises of our lives, the most important factor that determines the outcome is our interpersonal relationships, our interactions with the people who are close to us. For the greatest need of human beings, from the first to the last breath, is to make and maintain significant personal relationships. The ability to relate is the key to life and growth. This is also true in the other most important

* Eric Ericson, *Identity and the Life Cycle*, International Universities Press, New York 1959, pp. 56–7.

crisis of life, the process of dying. For the quality of dying is inevitably dependent upon feeling loved and loving, and on the atmosphere around the dying person, the support of those around him.

The acceptance of death will also be determined by the way previous experiences of great change were coped with, previous steps into the unknown were taken. Throughout life we have to learn to cope with loss, even in those new situations which in our society are occasions for celebration, such as leaving school or completing a training, marriage, parenthood. For on each of these joyful occasions there are elements of loss side by side with the gain. A denial of the loss means devaluing the past, and makes it impossible to mourn what has been lost. If such occasions become a starting point for emotional disturbance, this may be because the loss has remained unacknowledged.

It may be difficult to recognize that birth, through which life is gained, should involve loss. It may also be difficult to link the idea of loss with the very important phase of growth and development that occurs between the age of two and a half and five (the oedipal phase) when the child has to give up the exclusive two-person relationship with the mother and at the same time becomes aware of the differences between the sexes. The child's response to these differences may be experienced with an intensity of feeling that creates a fertile source of conflict for the child and often for the parents as well.

I should like to illustrate this complicated situation with a short example from my professional experience. A young mother came to see me deeply distressed because she felt her husband didn't love her any longer. He worked long hours, and when he came home he would fail to give her an affectionate greeting, but would go straight upstairs to their little daughter's bedroom and stand adoringly for a long time by the child's bed. After we had talked about her problems for a couple of sessions, this mother began to recall her own close relationship with her father (she was an only child) and how much her mother used to resent the affectionate games they played together. After this session she had a dream. She was lying in her bed as an adult woman and her father, who had died before she married, was walking round and round her bed, looking at her seductively. In telling me this dream she could herself make the link between her anxious jealousy of her little daughter and her feelings for her father. She was then able to talk to her husband about these feelings, and he, also an only child, posthumously born, then told her of his mother's possessive love for him and his own need to be close to her. When he met his wife he was glad to escape from his mother who lived in France. Now his charming little daughter had reactivated these early feelings. We may hope that this couple's ability to share their incestuous fantasies with each other enabled them to understand the great importance of this phase in their daughter's and in their own lives. They became aware that the parent, too, can only renounce the desirable loved child with a sense of loss.

Unresolved conflicts stemming from the oedipal phase are likely to be stirred up from time to time throughout the life-cycle, whenever great changes, especially those involving separations, become necessary. They play a great part in the choice of a marriage partner and in the interaction processes which develop between the couple. Whether the partner is chosen because he/she is like the parent of the opposite sex, or as unlike as possible, in either case, the relationship between the couple will reflect the emotional tie with the parents.

When I wrote my book *Death and the Family* and had interviews with adult sons and daughters who had recently lost a parent, I was very struck how often their oedipal fantasies had been reactivated by their parents' death. These fantasies may also become stirred up during puberty and adolescence when the individual has to give up childhood closeness and reliance on parents in order to grow into adulthood. At the same time he or she has to preserve a sense of continuity and loyalty to the family of origin. Adolescence, the phase when growth and adventure are most strongly experienced, although forward looking, can, therefore, also be a time of pain, grief and severe loss.

Until a few years ago, one could have gained the impression that change and crisis in the life-cycle stopped with adolescence. Now the mid-life crisis has been discovered and much publicized. Quite what it means, what brings it about, and even when it occurs, has led to considerable controversy: it has been said to fall within a time-span stretching from the age of thirty-five to sixty. What seems certain is that in our society, in which youth and youthfulness are so greatly admired, and sexuality plays such a large role, the fear of ageing and loss of youth is especially powerful. It oftens leads to depressive symptoms, or to a refusal to look realistically at the situation, or to resort to all kinds of phantom solutions, such as a younger lover.

In my work with people experiencing marriage problems, I have met many middle-aged couples who ask for help with a sexual problem, perhaps diminishing sexual potency. But underneath this presenting problem is mostly fear of loss. The children are leaving home, the couple have to resume their former relationship on their own, retirement may be looming with its loss of status. Parents may become ill or die, and the concern with death, which is now moving into the centre of the picture, makes the mid-life crisis different from all previous crises. Its outcome will set the scene for old age.

It is those people who have accepted crises of loss throughout life as part of their growth and development who are likely to respond in the same way to the inevitable losses of old age: the loss of mobility and stamina, diminishing senses, all sorts of aches and pains and the loss not only of contemporaries but frequently, too, of much younger relatives and friends. Bereavement in old age, the major loss to be faced in life, will be discussed more fully in Chapter Seven, 'The search for a meaning'.

In this last phase of life, more than in any previous one, the attitude to losses, including the loss of a future and the certainty of approaching death, will determine the quality of a long life. Now that physical crisis can often be avoided through drugs and medication we are in danger of losing sight of the fact that a crisis is a turning-point which can lead to increased health or to deterioration. It can make this last phase into the one for which all previous phases of life were made, and death into the final stage of growth.*

* *Death the final stage of growth*, Elisabeth Kubler-Ross, Prentice-Hall, New Jersey 1975.

To end this chapter I should like to tell two further life-stories. Kathleen, after a life of recurring loss, yet still showing perennial optimism, and Lilian, with her unfailing capacity to love, have both made positive use of their pains and losses and are enjoying a peaceful and loving old age. Some of the examples I will give later on, in the chapter dealing with physical and mental illness in old age, are the other side of the coin, showing how unresolved losses can lead to illness and confusion at the end of the life-cycle.

Kathleen is ninety-one. Occasionally she will sum herself up in this way: 'I'm not very intelligent, but I am interested in people—and when it comes to the people I love, I am interested in every single detail of their lives.'

Kathleen is, as she says, intensely involved in the day-to-day careers of her friends and family. She is an ardent sports fan, a follower of current affairs, a staunch Anglican and unashamed High Tory. She is also registered blind, though she has enough residual sight to walk about. Her favourite interest, reading, is therefore denied her—though she listens to 'talking books'. Her husband died leaving no money so she is poor and lives in a sheltered housing unit. It is tiny compared to the spacious home she has lived in—but it means she can be independent.

Kathleen's life is not easy. But despite her difficulties, she remains full of tremendous vitality. 'Do you know what has kept me going through everything? Only my infallible faith. Without that, how could I have lived?'

Her faith was 'caught' from her father, the central figure in the stable, ordered Edwardian family she grew up in. And her happy childhood she refers to as the 'backbone' of her existence. Her fundamental optimism and confidence in the goodness of life, other people, and God have been there from the beginning.

Her mother was a gentle but rather shy and remote figure. It is her father she talks of with warmth and it was his values that she identified with. He was a hard-working stockbroker, a self-made man with deep religious convictions—though Kathleen never remembers him speaking of religion. They walked to church together, the two of them, every Sunday. Kathleen remembers that at night her mother would 'just turn her head to be kissed' but her father would give her a bear hug. He had a great sense of fun: 'He would come back from the stock exchange with all these risqué stories and tell mother—she would look shocked, or pretend to be, and he would laugh.'

Her attachment to her father and to her younger brother, Hughie, was passionate. She has always preferred men as companions to women, shared (and still keeps up) her two brothers' interest in cricket, and before the outbreak of war threw herself into organizing boys' clubs. She was a plain girl, though then, as now, she gained attractiveness from her natural enthusiasm.

The greatest tragedy of her life was the loss of Charlie, her fiancé, 'my first and only sweetheart'. She adored Charlie with the devotion that before had been reserved for her father and younger brother, and with all the fervour of a passionate nature.

An officer in the First World War, Charlie fell ill with Hodgkinson's disease, was demobbed and returned home to die. Kathleen helped to nurse him and his last days are etched in her memory with an agonizing clarity. On the final day, Kathleen, exhausted, was sent to her room to have a rest. Suddenly she woke up to the sound of gushing water. (Later, she thought it was the water in Charlie's water bed draining away.) There was a bright light in the room and she saw the twelve apostles standing round her bed. The vision left her and Charlie's mother came into the room to tell her that a few minutes earlier Charlie had died.

This vision was a source of comfort to her in the following months. It was a glimpse of enduring life and love, a vivid reminder of a world whose beauty and justice transcended and co-existed with the desperate blackness of her present life. 'Why doesn't God let me die?' But he didn't and she would never let go of life voluntarily.

Significantly, it was her father who suggested that she might try to ease her grief by going out into the wider world and getting a job. She worked in the Ministry of Information and made fast friends with a colleague, Marjorie. It was natural for her to introduce her best friend to the person she loved best of all, her brother Hughie.

They fell in love and were to have fifty years of happy marriage together and Kathleen often quotes this story as an example of the way in which all suffering, in the light of faith, can be seen to have a purpose, a potential for good: 'Don't you see? Marjorie would never have met Hugh if I hadn't lost my Charlie and gone to work at the Ministry.' Kathleen also believes that God only permits those people to suffer who can 'take it' and that, through suffering, an individual can gain much greater empathy.

She felt deeply sorry for her boss at the Ministry, a man ten years older than her whose wife and baby had died on the same day in the great 'flu epidemic. Charlie had given her strict instructions, before he died, that if a 'good man' came along she was to marry him and have children. So when her boss, Bob, fell in love with her she agreed to marry him, not because she was in love, but because she felt Charlie would have wanted her to marry and she wanted to give this man another child.

They married and Kathleen became pregnant and knew happiness once more as she prepared for the baby's birth. But the birth was complicated and her son only lived for two minutes after the caesarian operation. In its way, this loss was as hard to bear as Charlie's death—not just because she was robbed of the child but because her motive for entering into the marriage was undermined.

Three months later, her friend Marjorie had her first baby. Kathleen's ability to bear her own loss was tested in a new and most painful way. 'One of the hardest things I ever did,' she says, 'was to go to Marjorie and take her baby in my arms.'

Three years later, the doctors allowed Kathleen to conceive again and she had one son, Simon. Married life for Kathleen was full of struggle. Her husband, Bob, had left his job at the Ministry and she had to pinch and scrape to send Simon to public school and give him the upbringing she wanted. Bob was often irritable and demanding—taking out on his too uncomplaining wife the frustrations and anxieties he felt at work.

Her son, Simon, served in the Second World War and

afterwards married a cheerful, outgoing Irish girl. 'When Simon married June,' Kathleen says, 'I gave him up to her in my mind. I'd done my part and he belonged to her.' Along with her love for her friends and family goes a firm belief that she must neither possess nor become dependent upon them.

Bob developed cancer and Kathleen nursed him through his long and painful illness. A few months after his death, her sight rapidly deteriorated. Reading, her greatest relaxation, now became impossible, though she was able still to move about a little. Neither then nor at any other time did she ask, 'Why me?' She stuck to her belief that there must be some purpose in her suffering. Later on, when her dying brother, Hugh, also became partially blind, she was able to tell him about 'talking books' on tapes, and arranged for the tapes to be sent to him, so bringing a new source of interest and entertainment into his life.

Meanwhile Simon had built a 'granny annexe' onto his house and pressed Kathleen—now registered blind—to stay with them. But she refused to lose her independence, even though to stay as a 'paying guest' so close to her son was very tempting. Her family has always remained the focus of her life. She had played an important part in bringing up her grandchildren, often acting as a surrogate mother when June took on a part-time job. She adores her grandson, Chris, and the recent break-up of his marriage has cast a long shadow over her late old age. Yet her life has always been a 'constant battle', it is not new to her to have to face pain, and now she has to face the suffering of her grandson and the loss of contact with her great-grandchildren. The thought of death and the end of the 'battle' is not unhappy, it is rather a source of comfort—all the more as she is convinced that Charlie waits for her on the other side of death. Kathleen thinks a lot about the past but particularly about those critical times in her life when she faced great loss. To look back at a period of suffering from her perspective of old age, and to see in it meaning and gain, is sure proof to her of the existence of a kindly God.

She is determined to enjoy what can be enjoyed and she refuses to give in to the temptations of 'acting old'. She is sure that some of her neighbours in the sheltered housing unit became confused because they 'gave in' and yielded to passivity, dependence and constricting self-centredness. She recently bought a vivid multi-coloured patchwork bedspread which she loves and describes as 'not the thing for a conventional old lady's bed-sit, but then I'm not a conventional old lady and never will be.'

Lilian is now nearly one hundred years old and lives alone on a sheltered housing estate in Hampshire. She did not have an easy start in life. Her mother was a dominating and ambitious woman who believed in the importance of getting on, owning property, and playing a part in politics. Yet she insisted that she did not want any glory for herself, but for her husband whom she attempted, unsuccessfully, to push into achievement. In his youth he was handsome and plausible, but without any ambition. He never kept a job, got into debt, and later took to drink. In the disappointing aftermath of her marriage the mother's ambitions were transferred onto her four children.

The eldest, Nigel, did not fulfil her dreams for him but, remaining a bachelor, stayed close to her throughout his life. Lilian was next, a beautiful child who grew into a most attractive young woman. She resisted her mother's ambitions for her, refused to study, and was more interested in boys and dancing. In her own way she was as wilful as her mother. Basil, her childhood companion, was his mother's favourite. He had inherited her strong will. When grown up he went to Canada where he married; he worked as a missionary clergyman and died out there of pneumonia.

During the childhood and early youth of these children the father's drinking became more severe, and the family's livelihood became precarious as jobs became more erratic. At times the family were very poor. There were terrible scenes when the father came home drunk and the mother provoked him into violence. She worked as a dressmaker to bring in some money, and the greater her poverty, the higher she held her head. Eventually the father had a kind of seizure. When the doctors told him he would kill himself if he went on drinking he immediately gave it up, and never touched another drop in his life.

Unfortunately, his wife never forgave him, although there must have been some sort of reconciliation for a daughter, Muriel, was born when Lilian was fifteen. The father, a reformed character now, made a great fuss of that baby daughter, and Lilian recalled with bitterness that he had always been too drunk to make a fuss of her. Meanwhile she had grown into a very beautiful young woman and was apprenticed into the drapery trade, where she worked her way up to become an important figure in a West End store. While there she fell in love deeply and passionately for the first and only time in her life with a nice 'gent' quite out of her class. He respected her 'honour' and they had an idyllic courtship, enjoying a moonlit romance among the lanes of June roses, until he broke it off with a letter. For Lilian this was a desperate blow.

When she was twenty-eight she became bored with work. The desire for children and a home of her own was so great that, since she was quite sure she would never love another man, she married a widower twenty years older than herself, one of the managers in her store. Financially it was a good match, but they had little in common, although he provided well materially for her and the two children. The children became all important for Lilian. She would have liked more but her husband, old enough to be her father, would not or could not produce them. Sexually, the marriage was very frustrating. He was a typical Victorian, a good citizen, good churchman, but dull.

Both children, Muriel and Nigel, who was five years younger, were completely spoiled by Lilian. This affected them in different ways; Muriel became a perpetual rebel and Nigel a clinging docile man who later married a woman with whom he continued the same dependent relationship he had had with his mother. Muriel married young, but her rebellious and independent nature, always in search of an unobtainable guru, could not be contained in a marriage and her husband left her soon after the birth of her son.

Her aunt Muriel, Lilian's younger sister, had also married young, a love marriage to a man with a TB hip. He remained a semi-invalid all his life and they had no children, living a quiet life in a cottage in Cornwall. After both her children had left home, Lilian felt the frustrations of living with an uncongenial man, so much older than herself, now deaf and ailing. When he died at the age of eighty-eight, Lilian, then aged sixty-five, started a new life by buying a cottage in Cornwall near her sister Muriel. Her daughter Muriel with her grandson, a second Basil, came to live with her and Lilian's elder brother, Nigel, also uprooted, found a house nearby.

These were happy times for Lilian, now the centre of a large family. But the question of young Basil's schooling had to be considered and Muriel thought it wiser to move elsewhere. Soon after she left, Lilian's elder brother, Nigel, died of a stroke and now seventy-nine years old herself, she felt suddenly very lonely. Her son, Nigel, stepped in and found her a flat near his own home. In spite of noisy surroundings and far from ideal conditions, Lilian once again made it into a proper home, ignoring all its negative features and enjoying what positives there were. Life went on like this until Lilian was eighty-seven. Then a road-widening scheme forced her to move once more. This took her into a brand new bungalow in a sheltered housing estate in semi-countryside. Her flexibility and home-making gifts made it what she calls her final home. 'I might just as well die here' and while she lives she enjoys it and all its amenities, as well as her neighbours and the friendly warden.

Two years later, her daughter Muriel retired and moved near her mother once again. Both grandsons, happily married and successful, have children, including daughters, and Lilian cherishes and enjoys the happy ending to her life. It is remarkable that although Lilian takes the greatest interest in all that her children and grandchildren do, she always guards her own autonomy. Daughter Muriel is deeply involved with religious concerns and her mother likes to hear about them, but says 'that is not for me; if I ever went to communion and saw a pound note lying before the altar rails, I would pick it up, so it is no good trying to be a communicant.' Basil the grandson, against all the odds, has made a good academic career, and is very active in politics. His grandmother is proud of him but says 'politics are fine for him and I like to hear of it, but I can see the cheating and hypocrisy in all parties and want to keep out of it.'

In spite of such critical comments, and in spite of the diminishing powers of old age and of her rapidly increasing blindness, Lilian is full of the joys of life, determined to make the best out of everything. She is loved by and loving to three generations of her family, helpful and friendly with her neighbours, and as the warden of the estate says 'an example to us all'. She is truly an example, in showing that a difficult start and severe losses and disappointments can help rather than hinder a fulfilled and integrated old age, through the all-surmounting ability to love.

When I chose the stories of Kathleen and Lilian for this chapter, because they show so clearly that the overcoming of painful losses throughout the life-cycle can help to achieve a good long life, I was unaware of the great similarities between them. Both had lost their one and only great love in early youth and both had later married, mainly to have children, much older men. Both are now nearly blind and live in sheltered housing with very limited material resources in contrast to their previously comfortable married lives. Both have the gift to enjoy every scrap of pleasure which comes their way. For both, the centre of their lives has remained their families of whom they are loved and loving members. The one fundamental difference between them is that Kathleen finds meaning and gain in her periods of suffering because to her they are the sure proof of the existence of a kindly God. Lilian, however, can only accept what she understands in the here-and-now situation of her existence. She is tolerant, and even admiring, of other values, but guards her integrity with unflinching honesty.

Other life-stories in this book (particularly in Chapter Seven) emphasize the help which a firm religious belief can give to old age. Without having chosen Kathleen's and Lilian's stories for this purpose, I welcome the opportunity to show through these two life-stories that religion, perhaps particularly in old age, need not be expressed as a creed in order to become a powerful formative attitude to life.

Although I have expressed my admiration for Kathleen's and Lilian's contentment in their materially restricted circumstances, I would hate to give the impression that I consider material support in old age to be unimportant. In our materialistic society there is, however, a danger of considering it the only important thing, and of allowing our consciences to be satisfied with the easier way of providing improvements in material needs, ignoring that the greatest need of old and very old people is to be acknowledged and valued as members of the community. But this will emerge more fully in later chapters.

CHAPTER THREE

The importance of the family

Love is the only sane and satisfactory answer to the problem of human existence.

ERICH FROMM, The Art of Loving

Whenever old age is discussed as a problem of our time, it is suggested that the changes in family relationships and the diminishing care of the younger generation for the old has made it so. It is true that the virtual disappearance of the extended family, and the emergence of the small nuclear family, as well as the frequent break-up of marriages, increased social and physical mobility, and the fact that many women may have jobs outside the home, have contributed to great changes in family relationships. These make it more difficult for married children to offer a home to their parents and/or grandparents whose life-expectancy has been greatly extended. It is equally true that many more old people than in previous generations can now afford to live on their own and choose to do so. They value their independence often even at the price of uncomfortable living conditions and recurring anxieties caused by being on their own.

These hardships are not present in the case of an old friend of mine. An almost blind, very deaf and physically handicapped man of eighty-five who lost his wife five years ago, he lives contentedly in his own home, cared for by a devoted housekeeper. For the first three years after his wife's death he was surrounded by photographs of her and lived entirely with her memory. He went every day to the cemetery, sat by her grave for hours, 'discussed' everything with her, and sought her advice on all matters. But as he has become too frail to continue these visits he appears bit by bit to have withdrawn from thinking of her. Now he never mentions her. Nor does he show much interest in his two married children and four grandchildren, beyond giving them generous presents. When his granddaughter got married recently he went to the church ceremony, and although he could not see or follow the service because of his near-deafness he seemed to enjoy it very much. Later a friend said how much he must have regretted not being able to see how beautiful his granddaughter had looked. He replied: 'What happens outside is unimportant. I enjoyed it because of what it meant to me inside myself.'

He stresses that he is perfectly happy. Although he is pleased to welcome visitors to his house with traces of his old hospitality and courtesy, he makes it clear after a short while that he prefers to be left alone. He says that silence is the most important thing to him; in silence he is near to God. Even though this man insists that his chief concern is his inner life, can one say that he has lost the ability to relate to others? Would he have withdrawn so much into silence if his wife was still alive or his children physically and emotionally closer to him? Has he given up relating to others because he has had for a long time no opportunity to practise it? For just as it is important for old people to use their limbs and muscles to enable them to continue to function, and to stimulate their intellect for it to remain responsive, it is essential to use their faculties to relate in order to continue emotional relationships.

My own belief, based on my own experience and that of many old people known to me, suggests that the ability to relate to others, or to something outside oneself beyond the immediate needs or sensations of the body, is every bit as important to the achievement of a good life in old age as it is at every other stage of the life-cycle. Old people are not a homogeneous group, probably less so than any other age group; their long life has made them individualistic. Their ability to relate, particularly to family and friends, is shaped by the events of their individual life history, perhaps by whether they have met with success or failure in the past, and also by their intellectual and social background.

Their responses to others will vary, too, according to their environment; whether they live alone or with their partner, with children, or with relatives or friends, in the community, in sheltered housing, or in some residential establishment. It will vary with the state of their health. If it is so poor that all their energies are needed simply to survive they may withdraw into themselves and become entirely self-absorbed. The behaviour of frail old people in institutional care often shows how hard it is for them just to get out of bed to dress and feed themselves. It is often all that they can manage to do. They have not got the energy to establish or maintain contact with another person, and are as unaware of the needs and feelings of others as tiny babies appear to be. Yet one wonders whether in spite of this withdrawal they are not longing, just as tiny babies are, to respond to someone who really cares for them.

In our time many people have married young, and life-expectancy is longer, yet couples who have reached their eighties together are rare, partly because only one, usually the woman, survives, but also because divorces and second and third marriages are no longer exceptions. To meet an old loving couple who have shared a lifelong partnership, with all the experience of caring and being cared for that that entails, can be a sheer delight. They convey a kind of unquestioning contentment. In his book *The View in Winter*,* Ronald Blythe writes about such a couple, Owen and Megan. After a long life in which they have given fully to their community, they have now pulled back from it and are living in themselves. Without the preceding decades of outgoing efforts on behalf of their neighbours, they may not now live so contentedly. The reason for their introversion is their need now to put all their energies into their extraordinary long marriage—which has lasted seventy-three years.

'Contemplating it,' Ronald Blythe writes, 'causes them to dwell on its beginnings, which in turn causes them to think of themselves as lovers. Ghosts of themselves as teenagers appear in facial expression and gesture as they tell a tale which rouses their own incredulity. Thinking of themselves when young, they intermittently are young, showing off and exchanging banter. A certain pathos breaks into the performance every now and then as they recognise that there is a touch of foolishness in their

* Ronald Blythe, *The View in Winter*, Allan Lane, 1979.

situation, and that people have a similar amused interest in them to that which they might covertly show towards unusually youthful newly weds. Time has put them on show. It has also caused them to observe the phenomenon of each other. They are both near to being a century old.

OWEN: How did we meet? We met by appointment. She was a student teacher when I first saw her—and what do you think I fancied about her first? Her legs. We went for a walk and we've walked hand in hand ever since.

MEGAN: I ought to have a medal for living with him. I think sometimes it's very wonderful to have had him all these years and not to get tired of him. It's wonderful, it is really. It is seventy-three years. And longer than that even, because we actually met eight years before we courted. He came to this valley to work for a fortnight.

OWEN: I stayed. I built this house.

MEGAN: When people see the photograph of him they say 'We can understand why you married him!' He is eighteen there.

OWEN: I was twenty-three when I got married. Now I'll soon be ninety-four. Twenty-three, ninety-four, but it's getting like a dream to me, being with my wife all that time. We've had our life but I wouldn't mind being young and having it again. The tragedy about human life is that it is so short. However long you live it is short in the end.

Mr and Mrs Frank, married for not quite fifty years, are another pair in whom one can delight. Both had to leave Germany because they were partly Jewish and, each the only member of their families who came to England, they met by chance soon after their arrival. Their professional trainings had been completed in Germany and they had now to try and re-establish themselves. They decided to marry a few days after their first meeting because they felt they could help each other to make a worthwhile life in this strange new world. By helping each other, with understanding and tenderness they achieved 'the gradual integration of two personalities so that each draws and gives to the other what he or she needs'.* They had three children who are now all married and successful in their chosen professions. Mr and Mrs Frank's ability to combine closeness with support for the identity of those near to them has enriched their marriage and their family.

Although they were uprooted early in their adult life and had to bear the pain of separating from their families, from the moment they built their lives together, through their efforts and their love for each other, all went well for them in their work and in their private life. After retirement they moved into a small house in a village where they have become respected members of the community. They share the work in house, kitchen and garden. Although the house is small they have provided space for the individual interests (photography and pottery) that each encourages in the other. Their hospitality is the delight of their friends. Thinking about them one recalls the story of Philemon and Bauces who after a long and happy life wanted to die together. The legend says that they were granted this special grace in return for the hospitality they had given to the Greek gods by whom they were turned, both at the same moment, into trees. Aware of their distinct individualities, they became, we are told, despite their closeness, two different kinds of tree. The Franks were delighted by this legend. 'I want to be a birch-tree,' Mrs Franks said, 'and he must be an oak.'

Mr and Mrs Croft are a couple who come from the poorest section of society. Having had only the barest of education, and having had to struggle hard all their working lives, they lack the resources for creative outlet which the Franks have always been able to enjoy. Yet they stress that they never expected to have such a good old age.

There is no doubt that great improvements in the lives of the old have taken place in this century, especially in the past thirty years. There were no old-age pensions until 1909 and although many more old people stayed with their then much larger

* Mary Stott, *Forgetting is No Excuse*, Faber and Faber, 1973.

families than do now, often under considerable stress for both parties, those who could not do so spent their last years in workhouses—institutional care in its bleakest form.

Mr and Mrs Croft married in the early 1920s and had two children. They lived in a village in Oxfordshire. Their small cottage had a lavatory in the garden, and they considered themselves very lucky to have running water and electricity in the house. Until the Second World War Mr Croft worked as a farm labourer at the appalling wages then prevailing, and Mrs Croft helped with the washing at the manor house. Their lives were simple and limited in the extreme.

The war brought considerable changes for the better. Wages increased and Mr Croft became an NCO in the Home Guard which increased his self-confidence. Their children had left home to start families of their own, and Mrs Croft took occasional paying guests, relatives of the soldiers who were stationed in the village.

Now both Crofts are in their late seventies and are in fairly good health. Mr Croft adds to their pension by a little work as a private gardener and raises some fruit and vegetables for sale on a small plot of ground that he rents. Their cottage has had a bathroom built on and is now well-furnished. They have a car so that they can regularly visit their married children and they participate in all the many social activities that their village provides for its senior citizens.

The life which Mr and Mrs Croft are now leading would have been unthinkable for a couple of their age and social status a generation ago. Now it is only exceptional because of the fact that Mr Croft started his life with severe deprivation. He was the illegitimate child of a soldier who disappeared before his birth, and his mother died in childbirth. His grandparents willingly brought him up and although they were very poor and very elderly they must have given him sufficient love and security for him to become the big, strong, good-looking man who has been able to create and maintain close, loving family relationships and a long united marriage.

Of course, by no means all long marriages are as richly happy as those so far described. Even among those old couples who have stayed together during their long life, there are many who hate the sight of each other. It is by no means exceptional for an old couple on admittance into residential care to prefer placement in different homes. And it is not at all unusual, on paying a condolence visit after the death of one partner, to find that the survivor is relieved and determined now to start on a new life.

It may even be found that an apparently good marriage becomes unhappy in old age. Mr and Mrs Kinsey appeared a very successful and popular couple when they celebrated their golden wedding anniversary. Although they were then in their late seventies, Mr Kinsey, an art historian and now retired from his university job, still kept busy writing reviews and articles and giving an occasional lecture. His wife, who had been a gifted and successful painter, had had to give up ten years earlier when her hands became painfully rheumatic; she remained very distressed about her lost creativity. Their son was married and had a family of his own. Although fond of his parents, his chief concern was with his own life and career.

Mr Kinsey had always found it difficult to make decisions and had depended on his colleagues, his secretary, and his wife to do so for him. But even when decisions had been made, he tried to find ways of altering them, and whenever anything went wrong, either in his business or in his personal life, he never blamed himself, always the other person. This attitude increased with old age so that it became barely tolerable. His more frequent outbursts of bad temper began to affect his wife. Her rheumatic condition was making it harder for her to perform household tasks with precision or on time, and whenever something went wrong, her husband's impatience and disapproval added to her distress, driving her into a state of anxiety and confusion to which he responded with near panic.

Eventually this vicious circle led to Mrs Kinsey's mental breakdown. She was admitted to a mental hospital where she is desperately unhappy. Her husband, for his part, keeps away from her as much as possible. He seems afraid of being infected by her mental instability and sometimes lets it be known that he feels it would be better for her and for him if she were dead. He feels guilty about such thoughts, and his more or less unconscious awareness that he has contributed to her breakdown so much overshadows his own old age (the couple are now both in their eighties) that he is unable to enjoy his relatively good physical health and unimpaired mental powers. It is almost as if he feels that his possession of these blessings is at his wife's expense. There is some truth in this feeling, as Mr Kinsey's lifelong projection of failures onto his wife was only bearable for her while she herself was well and creative.

By contrast, a couple who had a strained relationship earlier in their marriage may mature and learn to increase their tolerance to enjoy a more successful relationship in later years.

Mary Brown was the middle daughter of comfortably off, rather self-satisfied parents who owned a long-established family business. She was always one for the boys and her parents kept an anxious eye on her. Relieved when she became engaged to Fred they hoped, nevertheless, that the engagement would not lead to marriage, for they considered his family beneath them and of somewhat dubious social morality. However, when Mary told her parents a few months later that she was pregnant, they bundled the sobbing girl into a taxi, drove to Fred's home, and insisted on the earliest possible date for a wedding. Taking place virtually in secret in a registry office, this was a very different affair from the large and joyous wedding ceremonies arranged for Mary's two sisters. It was not a happy start for the young couple.

However, the birth of a baby boy was a great joy to the grandparents, for they had lost their only son in infancy. For Mary it was the fulfilment of her natural maternal feelings. Yet it added to the strains of the relationship between the young couple who had already started to fight verbally and physically. Twice Mary gathered up her son and returned to her parents' home, twice she was taken straight back to her husband. Her parents began to feel she had no stamina and came increasingly to side with their son-in-law. In due course Fred was taken into the Browns' family business and came to run it himself when his father-in-law retired. Mary, who had always worked for her father, now worked alongside her husband. That they were thus constantly together added to the tumultuousness of their marriage, which was held together by social pressures, economic necessity and an oddly compatible, rather violent sexual relationship.

In 1939, when war started, Fred, too old to be called up, volunteered for the army, largely in order to get away from his wife. Mary ran the business on her own, and the adoring grandparents were happy to take over the care of their grandson. Mary, now in her late thirties, had a casual affair with a serviceman stationed in the town and became pregnant by him. When Fred came home on leave, he demanded that she should get rid of the baby and arranged for a private abortion. He paid the nursing-home fee but stopped paying his wife's small salary from the business until every penny was recouped. His new position of power was increased by the fact that Mary was scared he would tell her parents of her fall from grace.

Soon after the war ended, Mary's parents died; the son, who had done well academically, went to university and never returned to live in the family home. Fred and Mary were now living for the first time as a couple on their own. This new situation improved their relationship. It no longer seemed so important which of them was in power, and their life went on more smoothly.

When Fred was in his sixties, he had a massive heart attack. The business had to be sold and Fred, now a frightened invalid, was in the power of his wife. Mary's natural maternal instincts prevailed. She looked after Fred very well and he exploited his new role of the dependent child. This situation improved the quality of their life, which continued in this way for about fifteen years. Then Mary had a stroke and Fred was devastated, terrified of losing her. Until then he had hardly been able to raise himself from his sickbed, yet when she came home from hospital, although she was less handicapped than he had feared, he was able to find unexpected strength to help her with shopping and household jobs and made her feel how much he cared. And so they live on, providing mutual support for each other. They have achieved a degree of unexpected togetherness only when they were both weakened in their old age.

Such interactive processes can be observed not only between marriage partners, but also between siblings. The emotions and ties of infancy and childhood remain the most important and binding in anyone's life although they are mostly lost to memory and buried in the unconscious. In old age the importance of early relationships is increased, especially after the loss of a marriage partner. Even those people who have a large circle of friends often prefer, with increasing age, the company of relatives who can provide links with their earlier life. The most important link remains the relationship with siblings because the original childhood relationship is fundamentally unaltered however much external situations may change. Although it is accidental whether a child is the eldest or youngest, the big sister or little brother, the role he or she has in the childhood family will affect all relationships throughout life.

This is clearly illustrated by the Pitt family. There were two sons and one daughter, Gina. She was the middle child, three years younger than her elder brother, and five years older than the younger. Their father died when they were all in their teens and the mother, a rather dominant woman, refused to let her daughter have a career, keeping her at home and yet making it clear how much she favoured the two boys. Although Gina obeyed her mother, their relationship was extremely ambivalent. To her brothers she felt close and developed a great sense of responsibility for them. They in turn spoiled her and listened to her advice while they remained single. When they both married soon after their mother's death Gina had to make a double adjustment. She found it difficult to establish a positive relationship with her sisters-in-law and after her mother's death was uncertain how to use her freedom. She does not seem to have resented her mother's preference for the brothers and on inheriting her jewellery used to show around, apparently with amusement, a gold medallion with frames for three portraits. The middle one had remained empty while the other two contained photographs of her brothers.

The eldest brother went abroad soon after his marrige. The younger brother married a very attractive girl and had one son who moved away from his family after leaving school, and one daughter who remained unmarried. She died of cancer in her early forties, a few months before her mother's death. Gina's younger brother was, therefore, suddenly left without wife and daughter and was naturally very distressed. His sister saw it as her duty and pleasure to give up her own life to look after him. Yet while her brother needed her help at this time, he resented being taken over by her and their relationship subsequently became very strained.

This situation was saved by the brother's neighbours and friends who were extremely supportive. A kind and helpful home-help was found for him and he adopted a cat who turned out to be a great character, and very affectionate. In these altered circumstances Gina was able to give up the fussing and mollycoddling of her brother, and he recovered his positive feelings for her. When Gina, now eighty-seven, recently said with conviction, 'My old age is the happiest time of my life,' she may have been expressing her awareness that at last she has been able to resolve her conflicting feelings towards her brothers and is now free to have her own identity without experiencing jealousy and guilt.

This chapter so far has been concerned with one-to-one relationships: husband to wife, brother to sister. Where an old couple is still seen to be at the centre of a web of relationships that extends down the generations and through the individual members to the community beyond, it can be quite striking how the pleasure derived from life remains undiminished despite quite severe physical and material handicaps.

Mr James, a bus driver for forty years, suffers from Parkinson's disease and is quite unable to care for himself. He and his wife, both eighty years old, recently celebrated their sixtieth wedding anniversary. They met in 1917 when both were in the army; Mrs James was one of the first WAACs, and Mr James a lorry driver. Meeting at a dance, it was love at first sight and they married soon after they were discharged from the army in 1919. Both came from large families. They went to live in Birmingham, Mrs James's home, and within a year had twin sons. These were hard times, for however much Mr James tried to get work, he could not find it.

In despair he wrote to the army major for whom he had worked in the war and who was now an MP in London. He immediately offered to recommend Mr James as a driver to London Transport if he could come to London for an interview. As it was impossible to find the money for the railway ticket, Mr James bicycled to London and back. He says the return journey seemed to be much shorter because he had the promise of a job and a small advance for the move in his pocket.

Within weeks the family moved to the north of London, where the twin sons were soon followed by two daughters. Money was very short and Mrs James had to leave the children with a kindly neighbour and go out to work, first as a cleaner and later as a school cook. Despite these hardships, the couple have never ceased to enjoy each other's company, and that of their children. Growing into healthy, happy adults they in turn found good, loving partners who became devoted members of the James family.

A big party was held for Mr and Mrs James's sixtieth wedding anniversary; they celebrated it with their four married children and their partners and with their nine grandchildren, six of whom are already married and have five children between them. Several of the grandchildren have been to university and have moved out of their working-class background, but remain lovingly attached to their grandparents.

Mrs James, who has to look after her husband day and night, has two widowed sisters and a widowed brother living in the same block of council flats who can give her some relief and help. The local council offers every possible help to enable the patient to stay at home: a home-help three times a week and a daily district nurse who comes in to care for Mr James in the morning. Mrs James nurses him devotedly but is realistic enough to allow herself an occasional respite, a small outing with her sisters and an annual fortnight's holiday arranged by the council. During that time Mr James goes to stay with a son who has just retired, and he feels that this is a change of air for him, too. Children and grandchildren have a visiting rota and there is hardly a day in the James's flat when one or other of them does not come to visit. There is always a welcoming cup of tea but if the guests want a meal, they bring it with them. It is this realistic attitude combined with a cheerful acceptance of illness and old age that enables them to remain content and full of appreciation for all the help that their local council is giving them.

The story of Mr and Mrs James helps to show that it is the inner rather than the outer world which creates a 'delightful old couple'. It also confirms the conclusion that Peter Townsend arrives at in his book *The Family Life of Old People.** He says that if children or other close relations are living near enough to be in regular contact with old people, offering them support when it is needed, but also enabling them to give help to the younger generations and feel wanted by them—then that is the best therapy for a good long life. How representative his findings are for other parts of the world (he is writing of London's East End) is difficult to assess, but there is evidence to suggest that they describe the close relationships that exist between the generations in the industrial north of England. There, too, grandparents now prefer to remain in their own home, and children and grandchildren continue the close regular contact which has always been part of their lives.

If for any reason the lives of old people lack the continual interaction across the generations that we see in the James's household, as well as in these others, then the danger may arise that they will withdraw their interest and concern from the community and those around them, for their lives will lack a forward-looking dimension that enables them to continue to relate to others.

The one relationship which is unique to old age—that of grandparents to grandchildren—appears to represent what all mortals want: the hope for continuity. It is not uncommon for a

* Peter Townsend, *The Family Life of Old People*, Penguin Books, 1951.

very sick old person to remain alive until the birth of a grandchild, and then die soon afterwards. It is as if the child is felt to be carrying on life for the grandparent, offering the hope of some sort of personal survival. Creative old people may gain this sense of continuity through their literary or artistic achievements, or through something that they have been able to contribute to make the world a bit better. Even the knowledge that a garden that he or she has created will continue to exist may help an individual to die peacefully.

The gratifications that can be gained through the emotional continuity represented in the relationship with grandchildren are most striking. A man of ninety-five whose single daughter came to live with him when his wife died is content and undemanding. In spite of almost total blindness and progressive deafness he has maintained his interest in the world. His greatest delight is derived from the frequent visits of his three-year-old great-granddaughter. The child likes to be as close as possible to him and puts her head on his chest to tell him stories which he cannot hear. But whilst she talks he caresses her and uses the same endearments for her as he used for his beloved wife. When his daughter commented on this, he said: 'Yes, she reminds me of your mother, to whom I feel especially close when the child is with me.'

Not only the need to keep the memory of a deceased marriage partner alive, but other needs, sometimes barely recognized, may be expressed in the relationship of grandparents to grandchildren. For example, Bernard's grandmother, Joan, attempted to see him as a replacement for her lost eldest son. Joan was the eldest daughter of a carpenter who had died when she was still in her teens, leaving her to care for her mother and younger siblings. Her mother, who became increasingly frail, derived much support from her closeness to her eldest daughter, who would therefore not consider marriage until after her mother's death. Soon afterwards, though, Joan married a young railway worker, a quiet, loving man by whom she had thirteen children, five boys and eight girls. Her eldest son, Frank, was the most precious to her, while her husband cherished most the second-born child, a daughter, named Theresa, who married at the beginning of the Second World War.

Joan's effort to give her eldest son a good education had been unstinting; in spite of great financial difficulties he had been sent to boarding school and Joan, a devout Roman Catholic, was delighted when he decided to train as a missionary. But while he was still studying he was called up for military service and subsequently killed in action. Three of his brothers later died in action, too. Joan was so affected by these losses that she had a mental breakdown from which she never fully recovered. Her husband, who had himself lost four brothers in the First World War, managed to keep her and the rest of the family going. Joan's only comfort was that her daughter Theresa gave birth to three sons. The last of them, Bernard, was born a few months after the death of his father, about the time that Joan's youngest son, Herbert, was killed within a few weeks of being called up.

Bernard became especially important to his grandparents, partly because he made his grandfather into a father figure, but also because his intellectual interests and some features of his character reminded Joan of her beloved eldest son, Frank. Just as she had with Frank, she encouraged Bernard's scholastic abilities and neither she nor her husband tired of answering his questions, especially when they concerned history and religion which had been Frank's subjects. On Bernard's tenth birthday his grandmother handed him the key of the livingroom cupboard where Frank's books had been locked away since his death. It was Bernard's first encounter with the literary classics from Homer to Shakespeare, and the boy responded enthusiastically to it. His grandparents' confidence in him greatly contributed to his personal development, which in turn enabled them to feel that, in spite of their great losses, their life was still worthwhile.

By the time that Joan's health began to deteriorate further, and it became clear that she had not long to live, Bernard, now twenty-one years old, had become his grandparents' confidant and it was with him that they shared their feelings of impending loss. After Joan's funeral the bereaved grandfather walked home on the arm of his youngest grandson. Less than six months later he collapsed on his way home from church and died immediately.

After the death of both his grandparents, Bernard arranged his life in a way which enabled him to fulfil their expectations for him. There can be no doubt that but for Bernard's birth and their close involvement in his childhood both grandparents would have experienced far greater pain and difficulty in coming to terms with the deaths of four sons. It is equally true that their unstinted affection throughout the time that Bernard was growing up played an almost incalculable part in shaping his life and relationships.

When the death of a marriage partner occurs in old age, it can be observed again and again that it is the grandchildren who are able to give the survivor a new purpose in life. Such a need can be overwhelmingly strong. In cases where a mother goes out to work, the grandmother may often be able to step in and thereby fill a need of her own as well as of the family. A woman, widowed when her youngest child was only one year old, struggled all her life in great poverty to look after and keep her children. When they were grown up she replaced them with her grandchildren, providing a home for them during the disruptions of the war. Then came the decision to evacuate their school to the country. Although the grandmother agreed that this was necessary for the children's safety, she felt deeply depressed at no longer being needed, and died within a few weeks.

A widowed grandfather, forced to earn his living doing uncongenial work, is now delighted that both a grandson and a granddaughter have professions which interest him deeply. The grandson is a cameraman, making mainly documentaries on social questions, a concern which the grandfather shares with him. The granddaughter is restoring old pictures—another of the grandfather's interests—and has recently been asked to do an important job in the grandfather's home town to which he himself has not been able to return since the last war. Both grandchildren like to discuss their work with him and make it clear how important he is to them. He in turn feels that they are fulfilling some of his artistic and intellectual ambitions, and that he is now living through them.

Many grandparents, however, are not able to fulfil their traditional role because of the uprooting of their families. Children and grandchildren have perhaps moved to another continent, where visits are impossible or infrequent, and grandparents have to be content with photos and possibly tapes of their grandchildren. Or the marriage of a son or daughter has broken down, the in-law has the custody of the children, and the grandparent loses contact. And if the son or daughter re-marries and the new partner brings children of his/her own into the marriage, grandparents may then have to come to terms with a new extended family, and with new grandchildren who may make a claim on their affection.

Grandparents may also be jealous of grandchildren: 'They have a better time than we did; too much money; not enough discipline.' In a later chapter, however, I shall discuss the often surprising acceptance by grandparents of their grandchildren's sexually permissive way of life.

The relationship with grandchildren is, of course, determined by the nature of the relationship with the intervening generation. I have spoken to several grandmothers who find it very much easier to relate to their granddaughters than they did to their daughters, and it is interesting how many of these granddaughters had chosen to follow their grandmother's profession, which had always been resented by their mother. If negative feelings have dominated the relationship between parents and children, they may lead to criticism of the grandchildren's upbringing. Attempts may be made to estrange them from their parents by spoiling them with presents and treats, and by trying to gain from them the affection which was missing in the relationship with their parents.

Grandchildren may evoke feelings of guilt and failure. Some women who have had traumatic experiences during their pregnancies and confinements may relive them when their daughters have children. One such woman, a Jew whose husband had left her before the birth of her only child, a daughter, had been dismayed when this girl at twenty had married a non-Jewish German and gone to live with him in Germany, the country in which her mother had felt persecuted and where she would not follow her. In spite of this 'tragedy', mother and daughter remained in friendly contact through letters and telephone calls and when the daughter became pregnant, the mother gained a new lease of life. On the daughter's eventual miscarriage, the mother had a mental breakdown and developed physical symptoms as if she herself had miscarried. She blamed herself, saying that she had always destroyed everything that she loved.

Many young grandparents, resenting the role that seems to make them old, behave as if they were their grandchildren's contemporaries, especially as they begin to grow up. Although this may give pleasure to both, it nevertheless deprives grandchildren of the important special relationship with their grandparents. It should not be forgotten that, in any relationship, the gain is on both sides: grandchildren may derive a sense of place, of knowing who they are, from listening to their grandparents and—particularly, perhaps, when they are small—from looking at their photos and mementoes and hearing stories of their own mother or father when young. Often grandchildren help their grandparents to feel young again, because they continue to relate to them as they did when they themselves were small and the grandparents younger and more active. I have been told, for example, of an adolescent grandson who dragged his, by now, aged grandparents up a steep cliff which they had climbed together ten years earlier, to enjoy the view. Other members of the family could not believe that the grandparents were still capable of the climb. That they did it, and enjoyed it, owed much to the feeling of physical support they obtained from their grandson.

The embargo on physical closeness which existed in the relationship to son or daughter is often lifted in the relationship to the grandchildren. Grandfathers seem to enjoy flirting with their growing-up granddaughters, and grandmothers may become agreeably excited when their grandsons make a fuss of them. I overheard the other day two grandmothers talking about their grandsons. 'Your Tommy is lovely, so handsome,' evoked the reply: 'Yes, I must admit, I quite fancy him!'

However, there are other reasons why childless women often remark that they feel more deprived by not having grandchildren than they did by not having had children, especially after the loss of their partner. Old people need the sense of being needed, to feel useful. They want not only to be cared for and to receive, but to be able to give something to others. Whenever this need is being considered professionally, the obvious solution is usually seen to lie in the grandparental role; where this relationship does not exist, attempts are being made in all sorts of ways to create it.

Children are encouraged to pay visits to old people's homes and help to entertain them; old people in turn are offered the chance to 'adopt' a grandchild with whom they can try to establish a personal relationship and do some of the things for them which a natural grandparent would normally do. In some of the Pestalozzi villages for orphan children in Germany and Switzerland, flats or bungalows for elderly couples who are prepared to act as grandparents are included in the planning. This can become an enriching experience both for the old and for the young, giving immense pleasure to each. It also gives rise to the hope that it will help the young to develop an affectionate attitude to old people, to see old age not as a disaster but as a rewarding phase of life, and therefore not to be frightened of becoming old themselves.

CHAPTER FOUR

Dependence/independence/ interdependence

It is sometimes difficult to maintain the right balance between an old person's wish to remain independent and the fact that all old people need at times of illness or special stress somebody on whom they can depend. Yet one so often hears of those who not only refuse all help but even refuse access to the people who offer it, probably because they feel that even the temporary acceptance of any help may threaten their independence.

A colleague of mine who was a social worker had a physically handicapped old woman, Mrs Smith, on her visiting list. She lived alone in a remote part of a suburb which my colleague had to pass on her way home. The first time she called she had to wait a long time for a response to the ringing of the bell. At last the door was opened a few inches, with the chain in position. When my colleague introduced herself as somebody from the local social services department Mrs Smith gave her a suspicious glance and quickly shut the door again without a word. My colleague did not let herself be put off. She called at the same time every day on her way home, waiting long enough for the shuffling old lady to get to the door. When it was not opened she would put a prepared note of friendly greetings through the letter box, which assured Mrs Smith that 'I shall call again tomorrow.' After she had done this for about a week she no longer heard the shuffling of feet after ringing the bell; Mrs Smith, she realized, was near the door waiting for the sound of the bell and the note to come through the letter box.

Unperturbed, my colleague continued her daily call a few weeks more until one day, when it was pelting with rain, just as she was about to put her note through the letter box, the door opened. The chain was still in place, but when she said 'I am soaked, may I come inside?' Mrs Smith opened the door and showed her into the kitchen, where the table was laid and a pot of tea prepared. This was greatly appreciated; Mrs Smith was the hostess, my colleague a guest, and nothing was said that was not appropriate to the situation. On leaving, the social worker asked when it would be convenient for Mrs Smith to see her again. Immediately she quite happily suggested the usual time, for by now Mrs Smith felt sure that her visitor understood her need to remain in control of the situation, and she no longer feared the loss of her independence.

This fear is the cause of much failure to seek help, medical or otherwise. Unfortunately it is often fully justified, since members of the helping profession behave as if they expect old people to submit gratefully to all that is offered to them. Their opinions are hardly ever asked for, nor are they supposed to ask questions.

One strong-willed old lady had been offered twice weekly attendance at her local hospital for physiotherapy. Transport was laid on for her and she was always ready in time, but before and during the treatment she insisted on putting what were considered time-wasting and annoying questions: could the position be changed as it was uncomfortable? What was the treatment supposed to achieve? How much longer would it go on? and so on. Her physiotherapist had a very demanding mother at home. She transferred her resentment about the mother to the 'awkward' patient and her annoyance grew to such an extent that she began to consider terminating the treatment. However, her senior, knowing something of her personal difficulties, luckily remembered that the same old lady had been successfully treated a year earlier in a different part of the hospital. When she rang the physiotherapist there to enquire whether she would take on the patient again, the reply was a joyful 'Of course, I love that independent old woman.'

It is worth asking, therefore, how often the personal idiosyncrasies of the helper may preclude an objective response to the so-called difficult patient. True in many situations where help is offered, this is most marked in those where the helper transfers on to the person who is in need of help her own feelings for somebody else, or her own fears about something that she is dreading for herself. In contrast to those cultures where old age is respected and honoured, in ours, where it is pitied and feared, most people dread becoming old and helpless. At a recent meeting concerned with the spiritual needs of the old, a clergyman present probably spoke for many when he said: 'I keep out of the way of the old, I am too terrified of becoming like them.' Even if not actually keeping out of their way, all too often members of the helping professions fail to take an individual interest in old people, which would enable them to get to know them, their life-story and something of their relationships. As a result, the old remain more or less anonymous and their individual needs are rarely understood. This attitude is perhaps most pronounced among the staff of residential homes, but to some extent it also applies to those concerned with old people living at home. Though it must be said that there are many who are unsparing of their time and devotion in caring for their patients, often their efforts fail for lack of understanding.

The widow of a well-known author had devoted herself to her husband while he was still alive. Although partly crippled and increasingly confined to a wheelchair, she had competently run a house, cooked, typed her husband's manuscripts, and read his proofs. When he died he left an unfinished book which she completed with the help of her son. In this way the publisher became aware of her capabilities and has since used her almost on a full-time basis for proof reading and editing. She earns her own money and has begun to live her own life, which includes travel, something her husband never liked. But as she is now a widow living alone, and is on the list of the disabled, she is frequently visited by social workers who suggest driving her to bingo clubs or including her in old people's outings to the seaside, activities that are all completely inappropriate for her. One of her problems is that she is slightly incontinent, and while she does not allow this to hamper her activities, it is nevertheless embarrassing. The health authorities supply her with the necessary pads and leave them outside her flat in packages clearly marked 'incontinence pads'. That her repeated requests to have them wrapped are constantly ignored indicates an appalling lack of sensitivity to this woman's need to preserve her dignity.

An equal disregard is often shown for an old person's need for independence. This is mostly done without malicious intent but because members of the helping professions, as well as the family, feel responsible for protecting the old person whom they fear may get lost, fall, or suffer injury in one way of another.

Mr Thomas was eighty-five years old when his wife died. Apart from the inevitable minor disabilities of old age he was in excellent health. His wife had been an invalid for many years, and for some time before her death had been unable to walk or even to stand unaided, moving from her bed to a wheelchair or a sofa. But she remained mentally alert, and even lively, and the couple lived as normal a life as was possible, listening to music, watching television, reading and talking, and clearly still enjoying each other's company. Their marriage had obviously always been a very happy one.

Mr Thomas had been an engineer in a partnership and had continued to work part-time until he was past eighty. Even then his retirement was due more to the fact that his wife's deteriorating health necessitated his presence at home than to his own unwillingness or inability to continue working. The couple had daily domestic help, and two married daughters who each lived about half-an-hour's drive away regularly visited them and helped them in many ways. Their neighbours had been provided with keys to the house and had promised to come running night or day if either of the Thomas's telephoned for help.

Until only a few weeks before his wife's death Mr Thomas had been alone with her at night and for many hours of most days. He had coped with the business of moving her about the house, getting her to and from the bathroom and putting her to bed, as well as dealing with all the necessary domestic chores. When she died, rather suddenly in the end, he appeared to face the situation with astonishing strength, recognizing that she had been ready and willing for death. He did grieve for his own loss, and made no secret of the fact that without her his life had not much purpose and he did not mind how soon he followed her. But this was expressed without complaint or self-pity. His family, however, were sure that the old man, while keeping up a wonderful façade, would collapse completely in a week or two. Friends and neighbours, less anxious and not so emotionally involved, could see no sign of this.

Yielding to his daughters' pressure, Mr Thomas agreed to go and live with one of them. There he was much loved and cossetted, yet after a month began to agitate to return to his own house. Every effort was made to dissuade him from this. His family felt that he could not possibly remain on his own and should either live with one of his daughters or go into an old people's home or a hotel. He refused to do either and returned home. Fond as he was of his family, he preferred intimacy at a distance, and he valued his independence.

His daughters, though, could not accept his decision. They took it in turns to stay with him at night and insisted on his spending all his weekends with one or other of them. Indeed, their behaviour put him in the position of making more of a nuisance of himself by making a stand for his independence than he would if he had surrendered to their pressure and become a dependent old man. Yet, tactfully, and without hurting them, he finally won his point and has now lived in his own home again for more than a year. He agrees that he can do this without anxiety since he knows that help is available should he ever need it.

While missing his wife's company severely he seems content with his present existence and shows no signs of mental or physical deterioration. He has many friends and relations who enjoy his company and visit him or take him to their houses for drinks and meals, and he goes out to the 'local' with his neighbours. He has no special hobbies and, except for technical journals, reads little. Superficially he seems to be a rather limited and conventional member of his class and generation, one who has always done the 'proper' thing and behaved in the 'proper' manner. Yet within this framework, perhaps protected by it, he is in fact a very special person. At eighty-six he has still an extremely interesting and independent mind and displays great perceptiveness and wisdom in his judgement of people and in his attitude to the generation of his grandchildren. They clearly adore him and enjoy telling him about their lives and activities. To visit him is for no one a burdensome duty, but truly enjoyable. Yet had he been deprived of his independence, he might well have turned into a bored and miserable old man, if not have lapsed into mental and physical decrepitude.

People who have always found it difficult to express or feel closeness or tenderness for others may protect themselves in old age from such feelings by keeping away from close contacts, using as a pretext for this withdrawal their need to preserve independence. A father whose wife had died leaving him with four young children never showed them any affection and kept them at a distance. In his old age he lived in great discomfort but rejected any help his children offered, insisting that to do so would make him dependent on them.

But there are also situations where the wish for independence in old age is used to resist what is felt to be exploitation by others, especially adult children. One old woman, living in a damp basement flat, nevertheless refused the offer of a comfortable self-contained flat in her daughter's house. She said: 'All my life my daughter wanted me to look after her. Now she wants me to look after her children and won't let me have my independence.'

In close family relationships it is often not easy to distinguish who is dependent on whom. This may be especially so in the case of a daughter who remains unmarried and continues to live at home with her parents. Miss Robinson, a civil servant, was the eldest daughter of a large family. She had always admired her father greatly, but could not get on with her dominating mother. After the father's death she continued, at the mother's request, to live with her, in what was a mutually ambivalent and often hostile relationship. At the age of eighty-five the mother became seriously ill and had to be admitted to hospital. During this time her daughter visited her every day before she went to work and immediately after she finished, remaining at the hospital as long as she could until the moment came for visitors to be turned out. On several occasions when the mother had pneumonia the doctors were doubtful whether or not to give her antibiotics but

Miss Robinson implored them to do so as she could not bear the thought that her mother might die. Her hope to resolve her guilt about her ambivalent feelings towards her mother depended on keeping her alive.

Any bereavement where often unconscious, negative feelings towards the lost person had dominated the relationship may deeply disturb the survivor. He/she may become depressed, unable to work through a normal mourning process and may only find relief for his feelings of guilt about not having loved the lost person enough by devoting the rest of his life to paying restitution, and never stop mourning.*

Even in a well-functioning family where much good will exists between the generations, it is sometimes difficult to be alive to an old person's wish for independence as was the case with Mr Thomas's daughters, particularly if this means that he/she must continue to live in poor surroundings. Children may find it particularly hard not to assert undue pressure when they can offer to their parents what appears to them to be a more convenient and comfortable home. They will have some difficulty in understanding their parents' desire to remain in the cramped, poor home they remember from their childhood, from which they themselves have broken away.

A Yorkshire working-class couple was securely settled in the community. All their children, now grown up, had moved away and had done well. The eldest son, an Oxford university lecturer, was devoted to his parents and they to him and his family. His greatest wish was to give them 'a good old age' and he bought for them a bungalow near his own house. When they came to live there, his family made them most welcome but they felt out of their depth and missed their neighbours and their familiar Yorkshire environment. After eighteen months they were so miserable that everybody concerned had to accept that it would be better for them to go back to their poor but familiar surroundings. Fortunately their old cottage was still available to them. In spite of disappointments on both sides, the mutual

* Lily Pincus, *Death and the Family*.

respect and understanding in this family was increased rather than diminished by what had happened.

The story of Mrs West reveals more difficult and ambivalent motives. She was born in 1903, the eldest of ten children of a drunken and violent father. Her childhood was one of extreme poverty and considerable misery. She went to school until she was thirteen but had often to stay at home to help with the latest baby or because she had no shoes to wear. From the age of eight she earned odd coppers cleaning steps, and went into service as soon as she left school. She married when she was eighteen and had a son. The marriage was unhappy. Her husband left her after a violent row, so that she had to support herself and her child by charring. In 1939 her son was called up and she was conscripted into a factory. After the war, she returned to earning her living by daily domestic work which meant a great drop in income, but she has always found the daily contact with the people she worked for a very satisfying part of her job.

Now in her seventies, Mrs West still lives alone in the poor flat which she has had for more than forty years. She has her pension but refuses to draw supplementary benefit. She has two charring jobs, one with a widower and one with a single woman; in both the work is light and easy, and she is much valued by her employers who are very grateful for the work she does and have made her into a personal friend. Her health is not good and her son is concerned about her. He has probably been criticized by other people for allowing his mother to go on working, and has pressed her to live with him and his wife, as their children are now married and he has adequate room for her. But she prefers her independence and says she cannot imagine what she would do without her work and the contacts which it brings her.

That Mrs West refused her son's offer and a much more comfortable life can perhaps best be understood if we remember how unhappy she was both in her childhood and in her marriage. Her charring jobs fill her need for friendly relationships in which she feels valued, without emotional commitments—which have caused so much pain in the past.

Members of the family or members of the helping professions

may thus have different motives for manipulating an old person into dependency. Equally, the old person's insistence on independence may express a mixture of conscious and unconscious feelings. Denying others, mainly members of the family, the opportunity to help, may be an expression of hostility, and may arouse in them feelings of guilt or anxiety.

Whatever the feelings which cause the old person's response to offers of help, they are likely to have their roots in past experiences. For the needs for dependence and independence are not only important in old age. They play a fundamental part in the development of each child, and are decisive in the conflicts of adolescence and in the pattern of relationships which the maturing individual develops.

The story of Bert and Connie is a fascinating example of how patterns of dependence were worked out in early childhood and, remaining unchanged, can still be exerting a powerful, and stifling, influence on old age.

They are brother and sister in their late seventies; he is the older by about seven years. Neither has ever married, and they are undemonstrative but devoted to one another. Their father, a professional man, many years his wife's senior, died when Connie was six years old. Their mother, of much humbler origin, was not altogether approved of by her husband's middle-class family. She was a resourceful woman of great character, and her influence on Bert and Connie can still be felt.

It is not easy to put together a picture of their early life, the boarding schools, the dinner parties and entertaining, the charming and beautiful mother who was also such an able, if eccentric, business-woman. One senses an element of fantasy in Connie's frequently told accounts of their good past. Bert, however, nods his confirmation of everything she relates.

Their mother ran a successful market garden in Hertfordshire, and her children worked for her. Connie will tell you that her brother was always a passive man who never took the initiative but left it to her to deal with any problems with staff, suppliers and customers. In her late seventies, their mother had a stroke and continued for a while to run her business through Connie. It is significant that Bert invariably refers to his mother as 'the boss', an epithet he also uses for his sister.

By the time their mother decided to sell her business to a property developer Bert was already past sixty and arthritic. They moved, hoping to start another smaller business but it never really materialized and by the time their mother died Bert was too old and crippled to do anything but look after the garden. Connie became head of the household and took up a door-to-door selling agency which satisfied her more gregarious needs. The closeness of the family unit, and probable earlier conflict, had isolated brother and sister from their extended family and they have no close friends.

In her seventy-fifth year Connie had a slight stroke 'like the boss'. She then gave up her 'job', and although not much physically affected by her stroke she is very frightened and very depressed—what will happen to him if 'anything else' happens to her? What will become of her if 'anything' happens to him? The more phlegmatic Bert seems to be surviving their predicament rather better than his sister, but her suffering both hurts and perplexes him, as do the spiteful attacks she now sometimes makes upon him.

Social Services give them good material aid, providing home-helps and other domiciliary services. Busy neighbours are kind but have their own lives to lead. Their material circumstances are good: a comfortably furnished home with hi-fi equipment, colour television. (These, though, are fairly recent acquisitions which they have been talked into buying to cheer themselves up, but are rarely used.)

In spite of her constant complaints of ill-health doctors still consider Connie fit to drive and once a fortnight, always on the same day, at the same time, she takes the car to draw their pensions from the Post Office in the next village. Life seems to be rendered possible by the maintenance of long-established routines. An identical breakfast is eaten every morning of the year at the same time. Then Bert gets dressed, completes his toilet and returns to sit on the same chair for the rest of the day. Meals on Wheels were offered and rejected because 'that's not what we eat at mid-day'. Lunch, consisting of a cheese sandwich, is the same every day except Sunday when Connie prepares their one cooked meal of the week. Bert may sit bored and unoccupied through a long day but only after supper (when the day's work is done!) does he read for a while. His routine is the more rigid and as he has always been a loner he seems to accept more easily the limitations and isolation of their lives. He can no longer walk unaided, cannot lift a full cup of tea safely, frequently drops asleep during the day and is kicked awake by the vigilant Connie, sitting always on the other side of the table. In addition to his prescribed medication he takes every night a mild laxative, a patent cold cure and a spoonful of cough mixture against getting a cold.

The once energetic Connie cannot reconcile herself to the restricted life they lead but neither can she see that those restrictions were imposed, in part, by her own fears and withdrawal from her previous community activities. She is embittered that people have stopped visiting them but the casual caller with ten minutes to spare will find that Connie, a non-stop talker, has skilfully manipulated them into a two-hour visit. If the visitor should call again on the same day the following week but does not turn up a week later Connie will be on the telephone: 'Are you ill? You always come to see us on Tuesdays.'

There seem to be only negative feelings in the household: fear of the empty life lying ahead of them, fear of leaving it. They cling to their fixed routines for safety and to the recollections of their past for reassurance of the value of their lives. Yet it seems clear that they have to idealize that past. The strongest feeling that they convey is of their interdependence, the roots of which lie in their early history.

The choice of a marriage partner is frequently determined by the need (established perhaps in childhood) for one to be dependent and the other to be strong and care-giving. Whether it is the husband or the wife who is the stronger one, usually both partners' collusive needs have created the situation, which may also be influenced by the cultural pattern of the time. In previous generations, until very recently, men were as a rule seen as strong and women as weak and helpless. It was then expected that women should abdicate responsibilities and lean on their husbands and later on their grown-up sons, whose task it was to spare them as far as possible worries and problems. Leading sheltered lives and avoiding all risks, such women often lived to a very old age. Discontented and demanding, some survive still, the last representatives of a generation of women who do not fit well into our present society in which married couples increasingly share responsibilities.

As the relationship between the sexes has changed in the western world over the last few decades, we are more likely now to meet an old couple where the woman is the strong member and the husband the weak and often childishly dependent one. Such a man cannot let his wife out of his sight and needs her constant attention which he gains through his affection, his pride in her capabilities, and his often chivalrous behaviour.

While such a wife may complain of being tied down and devoid of freedom, she has probably done her share to bring the situation about. She may have been a devoted mother to her children while they needed her, and as she needs to be needed, she now mothers her husband. Earlier in their lives his dependence on her may have resulted in a very satisfactory marriage but if, as usually happens, old age has made both partners less flexible, the collusive interaction between them may become a great strain. And this will become especially marked if the husband becomes disabled or severely ill and his will to survive seems to depend on his wife's need to care for him.

An old and sick husband may puzzle his wife by his obvious longing for his mother. I know of one old man who comforts himself at times when he is very tired by humming, 'I want to go to my mummy.' Whether such a need is more frequently expressed in a marriage where the wife is very mothering or very dominant needs further study. We also need to find out whether old women when they are ill and weak experience a similar longing for their mothers, or whether they perhaps transfer this longing to an important male figure—their father, their husband, their lover from an earlier time in their lives, or possibly their son.

In all the life-stories discussed in this chapter the complicated and often contradictory needs for dependence and independence were being worked out in the old person's own setting. The situation becomes much more difficult with old people in residential care where independence and individuality have to some extent to be subordinated to the efficient running of the home. It has been frequently observed that after admission to residential care, the condition of an old person often deteriorates, and he or she becomes either more angry and aggressive, or more apathetic and withdrawn. Such a change may not only be caused by the loss of his own home and the adjustment to strange living conditions, but also by his frustrated attempts to assert his identity and independence. As the understanding of the needs of the individual old person increases, we dare to hope that such painful developments can be avoided.

CHAPTER FIVE

Relationships with contemporaries

In a society in which more and more people are living longer and longer, it is important that every attempt should be made to understand the way old people relate to each other. In the past old people were seen, and in some country districts still are, as members of their family, rather than as the social responsibility of their community. Now a new situation has occurred, one that demands a better understanding of the individual needs of the old, and consideration of how they can best be met. It raises the question: how do old people relate to each other? The last decades have seen the emergence of distinct and often quite new patterns of relationships between adolescents and young people. Are the old, as the young have already done, beginning to seek each other out to form peer groups? Do they aim to win political influence which could enable them to change the living conditions that are often inappropriate to the needs of their age group?

To some extent this does seem to be happening in the USA. For example, there are Maggie Kuhn's Grey Panthers.* Among other things these locally based organizations of old people fight for such practical measures as easier steps to get on and off buses; longer intervals between changing traffic lights; and special shopping periods in supermarkets for old people, with cheaper prices and smaller portions. Several European cities have now started Grey Panther groups of their own, with limited success.

It is a welcome development, for quite apart from the fact that it can make old age easier, it can also make old people feel that they have a right to make demands on a community for which

* Maggie Kuhn, *On Ageing*, Westminster, Philadelphia 1979.

they worked and to which they contributed for as long as they were able. Such a movement among old people may help to establish the autonomy of their age group, just as that of adolescence was established some decades ago. The image of the old as tiresome, useless people may disappear if they are regarded as residents with a life-style of their own.

In recent years, for example in the leisure cities of California and other warm climate areas, some attempts have been made to express these life-styles in communities for the old. Often it is argued that these offer the ideal life for old people, but they undoubtedly present their own kind of problem, for such voluntary segregation means that the inhabitants are separated from the living concerns of younger generations, and these cities become a little like luxurious ghettoes. Frantic efforts are made to keep young, demanding a degree of conformity that denies the fact that there are as many different ways of ageing as there are old people. The insistence on youth and the denial of death may contribute to a state of anxiety, expressed in the safety measures that such communities insist on. Even in crime-conscious California these seem to be exaggerated. Many of the leisure cities are ringed round with walls, some even have a moat. They exhibit every kind of anti-burglar, anti-intruder device, as if the residents feel they are in danger of being attacked and robbed of something they cannot consider to be theirs by right.

In any case, these sun-cities, wherever they are, are only available to the wealthy. They provide no general solution to the greatest problems of old age: material deprivation and loneliness. The latter is most acutely felt in towns, where anonymity rather than neighbourliness is characteristic. This is one of the reasons (cheaper living conditions is another) why more and more retired couples move out of big towns into bungalows in semi-countrified suburbs or on the outskirts of seaside resorts. Many of these bungalows have been purpose-built for old residents, and form old people's estates that are within the means of lower middle-class buyers. Several large city councils are building estates for the old often on the edge of small towns. There, too, a certain amount of segregation is unavoidable, but without the aspirations for conformity and youthfulness found in the sun-cities. There is a general feeling of neighbourliness and support, and for many couples these estates do provide companionship.

It appears that they may also provide some safeguard against the increasing problem of excessive drinking in old age, usually connected with loneliness, especially after the loss of a marriage-partner. In William's case, for example, there seems no doubt that his increasingly desperate dependence on alcohol was the result of isolation. When he was in his early seventies he and his wife had sold the village shop that they had kept for many years, and they were able with the proceeds to buy a cottage six or seven miles away. Their only son remained in the village.

The cottage had no electricity and outside sanitation. This was not unusual in a rural area twenty-five years ago, and William's wife was a competent housekeeper and able to make life comfortable. She died five years after their move. In the eighteen ensuing years life became increasingly difficult for William. Relatives and acquaintances of his generation died; the reduction of rural bus services curtailed his son's visits. The only relief for William's loneliness were his nightly visits to the pub. He could be an entertaining companion, and there was always someone ready to stand him another pint or a whisky.

At home, conditions deteriorated over the years. To light a fire for cooking was too much trouble, and a small oil stove was used for heating food. Candles were substituted for oil lamps. The cottage became unspeakably dirty and neglected, although William kept his personal appearance for his nightly visit to the pub as neat and as clean as it had been in his shop-keeping days. When he gradually started to drink at home, during the day, the general state of neglect, and his neighbours' fears that he might cause a fire, brought him to the attention of the social service department. He refused any kind of help, but the social worker made regular visits, and was usually well-received by William in a greater or lesser state of inebriation: 'I should have gone when she did' . . . 'It's time I snuffed it.'

By now William was ninety-five years old, and life was without doubt a burden to the old man. Alcohol brought oblivion and absorbed a large part of his income. He ate little and seldom lit a fire, even in the coldest weather. A neighbour, seeing no light at all one winter's evening, went to the house and found William huddled in the dark with no heat. He resented her intrusion, grumbled as she lit his oil stove, and refused any help, saying only that he 'needed a drink'. For once he was quite sober. He was offensive when the neighbour called a doctor who, on arrival, found him collapsed in the garden. He died a few hours later of hyperthermia.

All sorts of devices may be resorted to by the old in order to alleviate boredom. Quite recently I was waiting in a queue at the pay desk of a supermarket. A very frail old lady who was waiting in front of me invited me to change places with her. When I protested, she pleaded: 'Please do; to wait a bit longer helps to pass the time.'

One of the problems for the community is to identify those old people who suffer boredom, as this old lady does, because they lack the inner resources that enable them to be alone. Those like my blind and deaf friend (see Chapter Three) who cherishes silence may be almost offended by the various offers to distract them. They are never bored or lonely, and so long as they have adequate physical care are happy to be on their own.

In recent years, social and religious organizations have tried to diminish loneliness by setting up social groups such as day-centres, luncheon clubs, and educational courses of all sorts for the old. Men and women who had a good deal of hardship in their working lives, feeling perhaps that they are much better off in their retirement, may now find themselves ready to seize the opportunity they lacked earlier for new interests and outlets. It may be more difficult for middle-class people, whose standard of living will probably have been eroded by retirement, to mix as readily in such groups. It is likely that they will consider them unable to cater for their intellectual interests. A man who formerly held an important job may feel that by retiring he has become a 'nobody' and will anxiously try to guard the status he felt he had in the past. He is likely to be supported in this self-sought exclusivity by his wife.

A solution to such problems possibly lies in the self-help and discussion groups that have been established by some London boroughs. They are usually advertised in the local press, are run by social workers with a special interest in old age, and are usually over-subscribed by pensioners of all classes who welcome the idea that they need not be just receivers of services, but can become participants in moves which may help to improve their lives.

How far senior citizens can make use of such groups will depend not only on their mobility and general state of health, but also on the degree of self-confidence and trust that they have gained in their previous relationships. The main aim of all these activities is to establish meaningful relations between old people and mobilize their abilities to be helpful to each other. In the last instance, it is the responsibility of every individual who is old to contribute towards a good long life for himself and others and help to further the changing image of old age.

This is more likely to be accomplished by those who live in their own homes, or at least within the community, perhaps with their families or in sheltered housing. Although contacts are not restricted to their age group, most of them are likely to seek the company of contemporaries, in spite of the fact that they are often critical and not very loving in their feelings towards them. This can perhaps best be understood as a defence against the symptoms of ageing that they can see in their contemporaries but dread discovering in themselves.

Most old people, especially those over eighty, have physical, mental, or personal problems which affect their lives. Their contemporaries have to choose between allowing themselves to be overwhelmed by demands for their time, help, and compassion, or feeling guilty at resisting those demands. The problem is especially acute when trying to help confused people, not only because they need much unhurried time, but also because the helpers may begin to feel that confusion is infectious, and to withdraw from the contact. Whichever way they decide, they have to endure the pain of watching old friends one after another become ill, suffer and die.

Apparently callous behaviour may be an attempt to avoid this pain. When the founder of a social club for old people suffered a stroke at one of their meetings, a local doctor took her to a nearby hospital and later returned to the group to give them news and comfort. To his amazement they did not want to talk about the incident at all. It was as if they had colluded to forget this woman who was a friend of most of those there. Similar observations have been made in the leisure cities; if one of the residents becomes seriously ill, nobody wants to know about it.

Yet, in spite of such ambivalence, relationships among old contemporaries prevail, for unless old people have children who they meet frequently, they have little opportunity to mix with members of younger generations. Often, too, they avoid such contacts because they fear the efforts, such as travel and entertaining, which may be involved. Or they are afraid they may be rejected or barely tolerated; they may be hard of hearing or unable to see well, and they may feel themselves to be out of touch with the attitudes of younger people. All this does not apply, or applies to a much lesser degree, as we saw in Chapter Three, to the old person who is sharing the life of his or her family and has natural on-going links with other generations.

The changes that have already been noted in family structures—smaller families, limited housing, women going out to work, and often two generations of old age pensioners surviving—make such a solution to the problems of old age increasingly infrequent in our western society. At the same time, many doubts and queries have been raised about the wisdom of providing more and more residential homes for the old. Not only are these the most expensive, but in many cases they are the least satisfactory solution, although for the very frail or confused they will always remain essential.

It has to be remembered, of course, that many still active old people are well provided for and feel happily settled in the kind of retirement homes, often in converted country houses with beautiful grounds, that have been founded for retired professional people. They can go there singly or with a partner, and are allowed to keep many of their treasured possessions with them. Various religious denominations also offer accommodation of a more private character to members of a particular religion. One reason for the success of such establishments is that people enter them, usually, at a relatively younger age. A limited number of them are supported by local authorities or by voluntary charities, but those which are not commit the individual old person to considerable financial outlay over an indefinite period of time, and are therefore only possible for those who have private means.

At present, however, the great majority of even very old people manage for themselves, supported to a greater or lesser degree by existing domiciliary services, such as home-helps, Meals on Wheels, and district nurses. The support of neighbours and volunteers plays an essential part in this attempt to keep people in their own homes. A good solution for those who either have not got a suitable home to live in, or are no longer able to live quite on their own, is the provision of sheltered housing with a resident warden. Some councils offer shared housing to a small number of old residents. If the participants are carefully selected and, particularly at the beginning, sufficiently supported, such an arrangement can be highly satisfactory, often surprisingly so.

In one of these houses, owned by a local authority, one man and four women are living together. The women take it in turns to cook and care for the man, and he, for his part, spoils them with little treats and pleasantnesses. He is in his seventies, still works as an artist's model, and makes no secret of the fact that he has an affair 'outside the flat' with one of the artists. This seems to increase his value in the eyes of his housemates, who share the excitement of the affair: since they do not have to compete for him as a lover they can peacefully divide the business of looking after him between them.

Until recently, sex in old age was not supposed to exist. Where it showed signs of doing so, it was either ridiculed or treated with disgust. Because of such attitudes, which still have wide prevalence, the subject has very rarely been discussed. Yet evidence suggests that sexual feelings, wishes and fantasies never cease. The few detailed studies which exist show that 51 per cent of men in the age group 86–90 years maintain their sexual interest, and that married men who continue a sexual relationship live longer. Old married couples who have enjoyed their sexual relationship can continue to do so for the rest of their lives, if their health permits, even if actual coitus becomes less important than the pleasure of comforting each other through physical closeness, caressing, touching. Mutual masturbation may be satisfying for some couples. If old women who have no partner are practising some form of masturbation, they often consider it as such a disgrace that they consult a doctor with the request to help them to fight it. Old men appear to be less troubled about masturbating, either alone or with the help of a partner. One widower, aged eighty-seven, pleaded after the death of his wife with a young relative to help him to an erection through masturbation now that his wife was no longer there to do this for him.

This uncle is probably what people call a 'dirty old man', a concept that tells us perhaps more about the general public's attitude to sex in old age than about the sexual manifestations of old men.

The few exhibiting 'park prowlers' I have heard of or come across were all younger men. I have been told quite a few stories of old men trying to fondle young girls, or trying to persuade female neighbours or passers-by to come and visit their flats, as well as stories of old men who like to tell dirty jokes. One of them upset all the women in an old people's club. When confronted by a social worker, he started to cry and told her that his wife had died a year ago, and that he felt desperately unhappy and frustrated. He didn't like telling these jokes, but it sometimes made him feel a little easier. I wonder how many so-called 'dirty old men' are unhappy, frustrated widowers who need to be understood rather than insulted.

Because of the silence surrounding the subject of sex, it may be that old people themselves fall into accepting arrangements that deny or preclude their sexual feelings or needs. 'For the old the sexual revolution came fifty years too late. They can hear and read about it, but they cannot touch. For they are burdened with the idea—society's and often their own—that sex is not for them.'* One woman in her late seventies, talking to her daughter, expressed surprise that so many of her contemporaries seemed to prefer single beds, or even single rooms. One couple she knew had made their two-roomed flat into two bed-sitting rooms. It must be awful, she thought, to have lived together for so long and not really like each other, even though she acknowledged that snoring and aches and pains might be reasons for some couples to choose separate sleeping arrangements. She herself had found that her need for physical contact and the expressions of love had increased, but it seemed to her that often it was easier for unmarried people to continue sexual enjoyment into old age.

She then went on to speak of a friend of hers, a professional woman now in her eighties, a much-loved and loving person, who had not married. For many years she had had a love affair with a married colleague fifteen years younger than herself. His wife had never been interested in sex, and had had apparently acquiesced throughout in her husband's affair with this woman, who was her best friend. The three of them went on holidays together, shared many interests, and were a happy triangle. The eighty-year-old woman admits that she still enjoys sex, and that it is its illicitness that is especially exciting to her.

So far as the question has been considered at all, it has tended to be assumed that a woman's sexual desire disappears earlier than her partner's. That it need not do so, and indeed may gain a fresh dimension in a situation of change, is shown by the following story. A woman who had had servants all her life, and had never had to move a finger in the house was sixty when her husband died. Without consulting anybody she sold her big house and advertised for a job as companion housekeeper to a gentleman. That was twenty years ago, and she is still in the job, working for someone she calls 'a perfect gentleman'. Her employer is slightly older than she is. When he wanted to marry her a few years ago she refused, but was quite happy to live with him as man and wife. Recently they travelled to Italy by train, and when she went to book a double sleeper in both their names,

* Morton Puner, *To the Good Long Life*.

the attendant pointed out that these were for married couples only. Although she was furious, she was obviously proud to boast of her unconventional attitude. It seems that she derives pleasure from thus competing with her granddaughter.

Another grandmother did this quite openly. When her granddaughter announced her engagement she immediately began to look for a boyfriend for herself, and loudly stated her intention to her family and friends. It seems that this woman was envious of the sexually permissive society, and was determined not to miss out on it herself before it was too late. Indeed, some degree of envy seems to be common among grandparents, although many of them find it surprisingly easy to accept the fact that their unmarried grandchildren are living, often for years, with a sexual partner.

Such envy is implicit, too, in the remark of an old woman who complained that a young couple in the flat above her seemed to be moving around all night in a creaking bed. 'At least', she said, 'when they get to my age, they won't have to wonder what it's all about.'

At day-centres, old people's clubs and other gatherings of old people, there is constant evidence of the interest women take in sexual matters. Recently observed: two old women, breathlessly climbing on to a bus and looking for seats. As one of them sat down by mistake on her handbag the other one, giggling, enquired: 'Did that give you a thrill—or have you forgotten?'

Another example from a council estate for old people shows the kind of excited interest that can be stirred up. A widow and a widower both in their eighties had become a loving couple. Most of the residents followed every movement in their affair with the keenest interest and attention; about 60 per cent of them showed pleasure and acceptance of the situation (why shouldn't they have a bit of fun?), the rest disapproved (disgusting at their age). What the affair very clearly provided was stimulation for them all. In the past there had been little interchange between the residents on the estate; now they all got together in groups to discuss the latest developments.

On the same estate the grandson of a resident goes jogging

early every morning dressed in very short shorts. Some of the old women always sit waiting eagerly for him to appear, the curtains pulled back. Knowing this, he shouts up to them 'Draw your curtains, you nosey old thing', which adds to their excitement and pleasure.

Yet the sexual needs of old women have scarcely been discussed or allowed to exist, while those of old men have been taken for granted. A husband whose wife appears to be uninterested in sex is likely to look for other solutions. It rarely occurs to him that his wife's lack of interest may be caused by his own attitude to her. He needs to seek reassurance that his fear of impotence, very possibly aggravated by his wife's coldness, is unfounded. One husband of seventy-nine only goes to see his GP whenever he has made love to some girl he has picked up in Leicester Square. He always arrives with a feeling of triumph. 'It was wonderful. I am still as potent as I was in my youth.' Having reported this he makes it clear that he feels guilty towards his wife, but 'she is not interested, so what can I do?' Each of his visits ends with the query: 'I wonder what my sons would say?'

Many GPs tell similar stories. The old men are mostly full of guilt and need reassurance that their sexual needs are not abnormal. To test out their potency becomes vitally important to them, especially at a time when they feel they have lost status through retirement. Their fear of failure may be less acute with a prostitute than with their wives who they fear will ridicule and despise them. They sense that it may upset the balance of their marriage.

An understanding wife can help her husband by taking the initiative in a way that is in keeping with their previous sexual relationship. She may be aware of some physical symptom, perhaps an infection, that is causing a passing impotence, and can thus reassure him. After all, intercourse is only one way of expressing love. Its failure should never be the end of sensuality; indeed close physical contact may gain increasing importance for them both, especially for the ageing wife. If she is ashamed of her changed body and feels unattractive, she may need her husband's caresses and understanding in order to be able to respond to his advances.

A vicious circle of lack of confidence can lead to mutual rejection. Yet if such feelings can be brought into the open they may not only be overcome, they may even form a new bond. If not, lack of communication may make a wife so frustrated and angry that she begins to suspect that the cause of her husband's lack of interest in her is a young mistress. One such woman asked for psychiatric help, fearing that she might kill her husband in her rage; she had found herself going to bed with the bread-knife.

About the sex life of old homosexuals, men and women, we know still less. They are likely to remain well hidden in their community because the social stigma which they have experienced throughout their lives is likely to increase when old age is added to their special life-style.

Two old women who have made their lives together are not necessarily labelled as lesbians, and are often helpful and much-valued members of their community. However, when a member of the Campaign for Homosexual Equality was recently talking about his cause in a launderette, a woman of over eighty came up to thank him: 'At the bottom of my heart I have always known that I am a lesbian, but I have never dared to admit it to myself and others. Now that I have listened to you, and have seen with what dignity you stand up for your cause, I feel how much I have missed. Thank you very much for liberating me.'

In spite of much publicity by a number of organizations, especially the Campaign for Homosexual Equality, male homosexuals often have to endure hostility and face great difficulties unless they are such well-known and highly respected people as Benjamin Britten and Peter Pears. After Britten's death Pears was able to talk on television about their great and creative love in a way that moved the world. I wonder, however, whether these two would have supported the increased publicity, and the growing number of clubs, pubs and agencies which now offer help, advice and companionship to same-sex lovers. I am discussing in a later chapter the particular difficulties that survivors of a same-sex relationship may have to face after the death of their partner.

A recent German film that starred Elizabeth Bergner, showing her in her eighties in an old people's home with her old husband of the same age, explored the theme of unending sexual longing. The old couple escape from the home for a day's outing which turns into a day full of disasters, but affords them many adventures.

In a crowded bus a young girl in jeans stands next to the old man; his battle not to pinch her attractive bottom, his final surrender, and his wife's obvious delight that he still wants to do so, is charmingly shown. By the end of the day the couple are completely exhausted and they fall asleep in an empty church in each other's arms, dreaming about their past sexual happiness.

This film is one of a number of attempts beginning to be made in film, on the stage, and in literature, to show that sex in old age has become mentionable. For example, *L'Angoisse du Roi Salomon* by Emile Ajar, due to be translated into English next year, describes the happiness of an eighty-five-year-old man who returns after a separation of thirty years and the death of his wife to a former mistress with whom he had been very much in love.

Even in real life, attitudes are starting to change. Everybody with experience of old people will have noticed that they come to life in one way or another whenever sex is talked about, however withdrawn and apathetic they appear to be otherwise. We all know that an old woman may get all pink and bright-eyed if a man, however jokingly, flirts with her. Such an experience obviously contributes to her physical well-being. The staff of old people's homes and of geriatric wards are beginning to become aware of the therapeutic benefit to both sexes of mixed accommodation. The ward sister in a mixed ward in a geriatric hospital said recently 'I don't mind at all if my old men touch my bosom or my bottom or even if they try to get their hands under my skirt, if that makes them feel a bit better; but what can I do for the women?' Although this ward sister's generous spirit may be exceptional, relationships between old men and old women are now beginning to be encouraged in sheltered housing and day-centres, as it has become evident that they improve the general atmosphere of the place. Both sexes take more trouble with their appearance and their manners, and often become more alive and active. As the head of a day-centre for very old and some disabled people remarked, 'Our site is conveniently next door to a registry office; I do hope our old people will make use of it.'

In the residential homes, too, the often punitive attitude of the past towards relationships between male and female residents is relaxing. Old married couples are encouraged to express their wish for a double room. (But not all married couples have such a wish; some even ask to be put into different homes.) Until quite recently it would not have been unusual, if a sexual or close relationship was discovered between two of the unmarried residents, for them both to be asked to leave. A couple of years ago an old man, invited by an old woman, a resident in the same home, to visit her at night, clumsily pressed the alarm bell instead of switching on the light. The furious matron let the bell ring all night, so that everybody in the home should know about the immoral goings-on, and then asked both 'guilty' residents to leave. Now it is perhaps more common for us to read in the newspapers of another Darby and Joan romance leading to the altar or the registry office.

Mrs Hill is one such story, proving that even very old, handicapped, or disabled people can, with some support, give great comfort to each other. She had had to cope with many losses and rejections in her life; nevertheless, and in spite of being severely disabled, she had maintained her sense of humour and general cheerfulness. When she moved into an old people's home she found herself sharing a table with a very depressed old man. On learning that he had recently lost his wife whom he had nursed devotedly for many years, she set out to do her utmost to cheer him up, and succeeded so well that they soon became a pair, and were given a flatlet of their own. Mrs Hill's physical condition had begun to deteriorate, but her good spirits were unabated. Her new husband again had somebody to look after and care for, and both of them gratefully enjoyed a new happiness.

CHAPTER SIX

Physical and mental health in old age

Age is a quality of mind,
If you have left your dreams behind,
If hope is cold,
If you no longer plan ahead,
If your ambitions are all dead,
Then you are old.
But if you make of life the best,
And in your life you still have zest,
If love you hold—
No matter how the years go by,
No matter how the birthdays fly,
You are not old.

Writing the title for this chapter I feel there ought to be a question mark after each word. To start with: 'What is old age?' It cannot be defined by the number of years a person has lived, as illustrated by the above poem by a ninety-year-old woman which came to me together with a letter: 'Often I find I am almost lost in the sense of forlornness and the feeling of not being necessary but then a flash of inspiration or the reunion with one or two friends enlivens me and I feel certainly old age should not be missed.' So while one can still enjoy such moments and can still feel love for others—perhaps one is not *too* old despite the birthdays. Some people are 'old' at fifty, others do not consider themselves to be so in their nineties. As Pablo Casals said at the age of ninety: 'Age is a relative matter. If you continue to work and to absorb the beauty of the world about you, you find that age does not necessarily mean getting old. At least, not in the ordinary sense. I feel many things more intensely than ever before, and for me life grows more fascinating.'

Such subjective viewpoints apart, there has also been a change in the objective conception of age. When I was a girl, people aged fifty were considered old, and were expected to dress and behave accordingly. At that time a friend of mine, an American psychiatrist, opposed this attitude by writing a book entitled *Life Begins at Fifty*. This was then regarded as a revolutionary statement. Now fifty-year-olds judge themselves and are judged to be young, yet they may well be grandparents and at the same time are perhaps having to cope with what is called the mid-life crisis. According to their personalities, this can lead to a denial of ageing or to premature ageing, but in any case, the scene will be set for old age.

How this will be experienced depends not entirely on subjective responses. Improvements in social welfare, advances in medicine and in living standards, have brought about great changes in the age structure of the western population and resulted in a spectacular increase in its life-span. How to cope with this newly found time of life is a social as well as a personal problem. Society has the responsibility of creating the conditions that make it possible for every old person to enjoy his extended final years of life. Ultimately, though, it is the personality of each individual which will determine how he/she copes with old age. Inevitably diminishing physical or mental powers are experienced by some old people as an illness that can lead to their withdrawal from active life; others may feel it as a challenge to make the utmost of their abilities, and their interest and curiosity about life will gain a new impetus.

Medical science can hope to diagnose and treat physical illness and promote physical health. Fairly good physical health without major physical impairments is a help towards a good long life, but it is not absolutely indispensable. Old people with all sorts of physical handicaps can lead a rich and meaningful life. So, again, it is possible to ask: what is the norm of good physical health in old age?

The World Health Organisation defines mental illness as 'All forms of illness in which psychological, emotional or behavioural disturbances are the dominating features.' Here, still more than in physical illness, the total personality has to be taken into account. And it is the total personality on which the shape of a good long life depends.

Once more, therefore, we return to the question: why are some old people rather than others enabled to live a good and even creative long life? What good fairy gave them the fundamental trust which enables such an achievement?

Let us consider again Pablo Casals' inspiring old age. We know that throughout his life he was devoted to his mother. At the age of eighty he married a twenty-year-old student of his and with her he enjoyed more than ten further happy years. He said she reminded him of his mother. Not only did she come from his mother's home town, but she had actually grown up in the house next door to the one in which his mother had lived. Pablo Casals' love for his mother and his love for his music were the source of his love for life.

But let us look at a few less eminent people. A jeweller aged ninety-three with a lifelong commitment to his craft felt such a compelling need to produce the most beautiful piece of jewellery that he sat up all night to finish it. In the morning, exhausted but deeply gratified by his achievement, he died in his wife's arms. His son, who speaks with great affection of his father, says: 'We could not wish anything better for him. All his life he lived for the beauty of his work and was never interested in money.'

A Scottish school inspector who died when he was one hundred and two had walked until a few months before his death across the Scottish hills to visit the schools and the children whom he felt needed him. His deep interest in the schools and the children whom he had served all his life and his love for them gave him the strength to achieve this.

A single woman, Miss Grant, celebrated her hundredth birthday with a circle of friends and neighbours. It was a happy occasion. She was the eldest of five siblings and had been considered the most delicate of them but had survived them all. Her father, the owner of a small shop, died when she was eight. Her mother took over the shop to keep her children. Miss Grant left school at fourteen to help her mother, against her teachers' advice: they felt she had a chance of gaining a scholarship to university. She did not consider this as a sacrifice but enjoyed life and the friendship of her neighbours. She was popular and had several suitors, but had never thought of marrying and leaving her mother. The two of them ran the shop and the household together. Her mother died in 1926 and Miss Grant carried on the shop without her for another ten years before selling it. The proceeds bought a house for her and her two single sisters. She continued to look after them until they died.

It is the same house in which Miss Grant recently celebrated her hundredth birthday. She is still a member of the Conservative Party and goes to church on Sundays if the weather allows. But the really important thing for her is her friendship with neighbours and her remaining relatives. One of them, a distant cousin, parks his car in her drive. He pretends that he cannot find another parking space but in reality it allows him to keep an eye on the old lady, a much valued member of her community. She says she has never had any doubts about the right thing to do and has therefore never had any regrets in her life.

Another family of four sisters, now all aged between eighty and ninety, have remained actively involved in all sorts of community services and lovingly united with each other. When the eldest sister celebrated her ninetieth birthday, they gave a joint thanksgiving party for forty-three younger members of their extended families, and in their speeches on that festive occasion stressed that they drew their strength for their active old lives from their roots in their community and from their faith.

I could recount many more examples of ordinary, very old people who have continued to make valuable contributions to their community. There is the ninety-two-year-old gardener who still cares for his neighbours. They trustingly turn to him in all emergencies, and he responds competently and joyfully when they need help in the garden, or with small jobs in the house, or with baby-sitting, or looking after their houses and pets when they go on holidays. There is the ninety-year-old farmer's widow who helps her son in the fields from dawn to dusk just as she helped her husband in the past.

There are doctors, psychotherapists, analysts in their eighties and nineties (Anna Freud, Freud's daughter is one of them) who continue to be a lifeline for their patients and make valuable contributions to further studies. I know personally of a ninety-year-old physiotherapist who not only continues to teach and treat patients, but has recently travelled abroad at the invitation of a university clinic to give a course on her special methods.

Innumerable very old people remain deeply committed to society and to social and political causes. Their lifelong experience and enthusiasm is of great help to their parties and movements. In the nuclear disarmament movement, for example, several members of over eighty are among the most tireless marchers and the most convincing canvassers.

All these examples suggest that the best recipe for a good long life is continued zest and curiosity, and a way of life that enables old people to feel valued and cared for, as well as caring for others. The sheer number of people who now live into a very old age (a hundredth birthday is no longer exceptional) goes beyond any previous experience. The situation is all the more complex and baffling because this generation of the old is a generation of survivors from the hardships and stresses of two world wars. For many this involved being driven away from their homes, required adjustment to tremendous changes in all areas of life, and very often to great personal losses. Others were prisoners of war for many years, or interned in Europe or Korea. Even if they were not themselves holocaust-victims, today's old people have had to live under the shadow of cruelty on an unimaginable scale, and since the war have had to come to terms with Hiroshima and the constant nuclear threat.

How has all this affected the survivors? What physical and mental abilities have made it possible for them to reach such an exceptional old age in spite of all these stresses, to which so many others have succumbed? We know that they had developed extraordinary survival skills as well as suffering traumas. In recent years it has been acknowledged that many of those who suffered persecution under the Nazi regime, yet have appeared to be well adjusted and established in often highly successful careers set up after emigration, have become after retirement and in old age very disturbed, showing severe symptoms of persecution anxieties. It seems that as long as they felt secure in their positions of success they could keep traumatic experiences at bay, but were overwhelmed by them once they had lost that security. We also know that the survivors of concentration camps are often burdened with feelings of guilt. Why should they have survived when millions, among them often their nearest and dearest, perished? Their eternal question: why was I saved?—what debt do I owe for my life? is one of the prices they pay.*

Moreover, this generation of old people is doubly burdened. Not only do they have to carry the responsibility of having survived when so many of their contemporaries have perished; at the same time they have lost the prestige of old age. The respect which was paid to previous generations of the old, and is still paid to them in some eastern cultures, compensated for diminishing abilities. To give back to old people a sense of their own value will not only make them healthier and happier, but will enable them, as the stories recounted earlier demonstrate, to contribute to society their talents and their experiences of a long life.

The community can help towards such an achievement only if it increases its awareness that medical and social improvements are not enough. They have to be matched by greater understanding of the emotional needs of the old, the greatest of which is to feel wanted. Though many within the caring professions, voluntary organizations and churches are aware of this need and keen to foster ways of answering it, society as a whole, regarding old people still as tiresome and useless, treats them as irresponsible and compels their dependence. The feeling of helplessness experienced by the old is being increased by the fact that they have become in many ways victims of exploitation.

I have recently been involved with the plight of an eighty-six-

*The response of concentration-camp survivors has been studied by many authors, among them Bruno Bettelheim, *Surviving*, Thames and Hudson, 1979, and Helen Epstein, *Children of the Holocaust*, G. P. Putnam & Sons, New York 1979.

year-old friend that illustrates this. For twenty years she has lived in a rented flat. During this time all the other flats in the block have been sold to the residents. My friend is a very undemanding, helpful person, and has been in good health until a few months ago, when an attack of shingles made her less mobile and undermined her self-confidence. When she was summoned to a hospital department, she naturally assumed it would be for further treatment. Instead it emerged that they had to inform her that a letter had been received suggesting that she was neglecting herself, and her flat, and was no longer fit to live on her own. Fortunately it could be proved that not a word of these accusations, which were made by the landlord who wants to sell the flat, was true. When I informed the social service department of this incident I was told that they are only too familiar with such situations, which are becoming more frequent. Even if, as in the case of my friend, the landlord has no legal chance of pressing his case, such accusations can upset and harass old people to such a degree that they have a mental breakdown and have to be taken into care. My friend has been so upset by the threat of losing her flat that she has completely lost her previous zest for life, and needs every support in order to regain some of her balance.

Another fear which undermines old people's health and self-confidence is of being robbed and attacked. Again and again one hears or reads stories of old people's handbags being snatched from them, or of them being kicked down, 'just for the fun of it' as a gang of youngsters said. A recent television programme with the title 'They can't run fast enough' raised considerable concern. The media was accused of exaggerating the situation and making old people afraid to go out. Paradoxically, the greater vulnerability of the old is partly caused by the positive fact that they are now, to a much greater degree than in the past, living on their own, and leading more independent lives.

A very active seventy-seven-year-old friend of mine has just returned from a visit to China. She was full of enthusiasm for all she had seen; her only complaint was that she was never allowed to cross a road or to climb a few steps without some young person hurrying to help her. Her comment was: 'What a nuisance, I don't need that.' How different from our situation where old people are not revered, but seen as helpless victims. This can only add to their depression, exacerbating a feeling that their life, as it draws to its end, has been useless; or they are leaving nothing of value behind.

Those who offer genuine interest to an old individual can be deeply gratified to observe the great improvement to their health and well-being which this concern brings about. For example, to encourage a depressed and withdrawn old person to talk about his or her life and relationships may lead to quite surprising changes. Experiments with the taping of such interviews and playing them back to the old person have proved to be of surprising therapeutic effectiveness. Listening to the tape together and showing appreciative interest gives new value to the life, and the fact that the tapes can be heard again and again by friends, children and grandchildren provides a permanent testimony.

One very depressed old woman, completely withdrawn from life, was played the tape of her life-story. After listening to it, she was encouraged to join an occupational therapy group and subsequently made a rug that won a prize in an exhibition. Her creativity, her investment in life, had been renewed.

When I spoke of the effectiveness of these taped interviews to a friend of mine who is a historian, he tended to play down my enthusiasm. Such interviews with old people, he said, had for some time been used to build up historical archives. There was nothing new in them. However, a fortnight later he 'phoned to tell me that after our meeting he had gone with a team to interview an old man who was so frail and depressed that it seemed an imposition to worry him. All the same they went ahead, and not only did the old man not appear to mind, but he looked rather better after the interview than he had before. A week later my friend 'phoned him to inquire how he was and was told: 'I don't quite know why, but since your visit I have been feeling much better.' Telling me this story, my friend added: 'Perhaps I conducted this interview more with a therapeutic than with a historical approach.'

The permanency of the tape seems to have a great value, even though the term therapeutic or even psycho-therapeutic may be rather misleading; all I mean to convey is the importance of the attempt to understand the old person as an individual rather than to regard him or her as an anonymous old creature. It is mainly the empathy which is therapeutic.

One frail old lady in a nursing home was quite happy and co-operative until her family arranged for her to be moved from her room on the second-floor to a ground-floor room so that she could use the garden. It was a nice enough room, but far from being happy she became extremely distressed. She could not sleep and every night rang for the night nurse, but could not explain what was bothering her. The staff had begun to consider moving her to a psychiatric hospital when a young social worker offered to spend some time with the old lady to find out what was upsetting her. At first her attempts were met only with despair and the patient's inability to express the cause of her distress. Slowly, however, it emerged that she was missing the sound of bells. All her life she had heard the hourly ringing of bells; in the second-floor room she had been able to hear them too and had been comforted by them in the strangeness of her surroundings. But in the ground-floor room she could not hear them, and she felt completely lost. When a chiming clock was supplied in her room, she settled down happily again. But for the understanding of a caring social worker, she might well have ended her life as a psychiatric patient.

It is because of such experiences that I feel justified in stressing yet again that the understanding of old people's individual needs and characteristics is paramount. The emphasis that in the past has been, and in many homes still is, laid on cleanliness, tidiness and strict timetables, seems inappropriate and may be frightening to an old person, who may have particular difficulties in maintaining them. One geriatric consultant told me of an ambitious and highly efficient ward sister who ran a meticulously kept ward. All the patients looked very well cared for, the food was excellent and well served, but eighty per cent of the patients were incontinent, fifty per cent were unable to feed themselves, and all of them appeared anxious and worried. The fact that they were treated like irresponsible children, called by their Christian names and reprimanded as 'naughty boy' or 'naughty girl', had reduced them to the status of frightened children.

At the first possible opportunity the 'perfect' ward sister was replaced by a less rigid one, and the other staff members were offered weekly discussion groups, in which they began to understand the importance of taking an individual interest in their patients. Four months after these changes all the patients were able to feed themselves, only a very few remained incontinent, and the altered atmosphere in the ward had made everybody, patients and staff, much happier.

The lessons from this experience cannot be emphasized strongly enough. A very kind but business-like matron recently showed me round her beautifully kept hospital. She opened the last door saying, 'And here you see our darling babies.' What I saw were old ladies in cots, spotlessly clean and nicely dressed, with carefully arranged hair-dos, many of them with ribbons. They were all smiling, because that is what is expected of 'darling babies', but in contrast to babies they were not allowed to risk any attempt at independence.

In another geriatric hospital where I was shown round a ward of very regressed patients everything was also done for them as if they were tiny babies. But the difference was that there was always an accompanying expression of hope that the patients would become stronger and more independent, and they were given every encouragement to try to achieve this. Such an approach to old feeble patients is very time-consuming for the nursing staff, much more so than it would be to simply treat them as babies. At the end of my visit I was taken to see the bungalows in the hospital grounds where four or five patients who had been as regressed on admission as those I had seen in the wards were now living. With some support they were able to look after themselves and each other, and it became clear to me how helpful to the patients—in the long run—how time-saving and rewarding for the staff the hospital policy of encouraging independence can be. Of course, not all regressed old patients will respond so successfully to such expectations, but I was assured that a large proportion of them do.

The emphasis in such 'therapeutic' wards, in which the patient is given some responsibility for his own recovery, is placed on the effort to understand the individual, his life-story and his relationships, and on the recognition of his value as an autonomous human being. With this goes new knowledge about the treatability of some old-age disorders. Such new knowledge is beginning to help to distinguish more clearly between physical, mental and psychological causes of confusion, and has led to the recognition that many of them are curable. This affects not only the attitude of old people to their symptoms; but also the attitude of doctors and nursing staff to their work. Younger members of the profession, in a spirit of enthusiasm and hope, are now choosing geriatric work that has hitherto often been regarded as hopeless; and with this goes a slow change in the negative image of old age.

The importance of a relaxed atmosphere in helping old people in residential care to relate to each other is self-evident, but may require some change in the planning of living-rooms. The nightmare of rows of desperately lonely, angry old people sitting along the walls in gloomy silence staring at the television without seeing anything remains the scene in many establishments. If large rooms cannot be subdivided, chairs might be arranged in small groups around tables to encourage social intercourse. Surprisingly, this is often resisted by patients and staff alike. Yet whenever an occupational therapist or another staff member can show a personal involvement and work or chat with a small group of residents, without expecting any special 'performance', the whole atmosphere often improves considerably.

Especially confused people respond much better to such a personal approach than they would to intellectual or technical instruction. When I visited a very confused woman in her old-age home I found her playing unhappily with the knobs of a bed-side table, muttering over and over again, 'I don't know what to do, I don't know whether to turn the knobs up or down.' She was so agitated that she was unable to absorb my greeting, or show awareness of the flowers I had brought her. To try and understand what it was that was worrying her I said that it seemed to me that she was upset by something in the home but was not quite sure whether she could change it. At once her feelings became clearer, and she mentioned what had annoyed her, concluding that things were not too bad and it was best to leave them as they were. My realization that the larger problem existed enabled her to think about the situation in a more positive way, and to my delight she was able within a few minutes to offer help, happily and efficiently, to another resident who could not get out of her chair.

The greatest despair of old people, which they often deny out of pride or hopelessness, is caused by loneliness (already touched on in Chapter Five). It affects both those who live in their own homes and those in residential care, and its often warping and unbalancing effects can only be relieved through sympathetic understanding. Without such understanding, the most well-meaning attempts to counteract loneliness by social arrangements, such as the day-centres, clubs or outings mentioned earlier, are likely to be defeated.

One way that an old person deprived of an actual continuing relationship may cope with the despair of loneliness is to live with an imaginary one. Miss Field, aged eighty-seven, is a long-stay patient in a geriatric hospital. She is very attached to the nurse who looks after her who has found out that Miss Field lives with the memory of her fiancé, killed in the First World War. In her mind he is always with her, and her nurse has got used to including him in whatever she is doing with or for her patient. 'George would like you to go for a little walk', or 'George always wanted you to have a hot drink at night.' Assured by the frequent mention of his name, Miss Field is happy and co-operative. But when her nurse had to go on sick leave without being able to tell her colleagues about George, Miss Field became so angry and obstructive that she upset everybody on the ward and the staff were at a loss what to do. Fortunately, before the situation got completely out of hand, the understanding nurse returned and was quickly able to restore Miss Field's feeling of safety which depends on her fantasy being given the validity of some recognition by another person. Miss Field is one of many people who live with an internalized relationship which for them becomes an aid for survival.

The subject of the fantasy is not always one of love. Miss Brent, who was terribly crippled, could never forgive her sister Peggy for having been pretty, having had boy friends, and for having married. She liked to tell 'terrible' sexual stories about this sister and her husband, and her own sexual frustrations seemed to get some outlet from her endless recounting of lurid stories about sexual carryings-on. These could be stimulated by anything and reached a pitch of obsession when she once found in a Butlins Holiday camp an old man using the lavatory clearly marked 'Lassies'. The way Miss Brent went on talking about sex seemed sometimes to border on madness, yet it was in some way therapeutic since it seemed to help her to tolerate her own frustrated and sad life.

Mr Graham, too, seemed to survive a lonely and disappointed life through his fantasies. A compassionate woman had noticed him sitting for hours on end over a warm grating in a church, looking grubby and ragged. It was obvious from his appearance that he was sleeping rough. She gave him shelter and helped him to recover, and gradually it emerged that he was an intelligent, well-educated man who could speak Latin and Greek. He never talked about his life, and what had led to his utter breakdown remained a mystery. He did not seem to have any relationships and once said he could feel nothing for anybody. 'I have locked my heart and thrown away the key.' Only after his death did it emerge that he had once been married and divorced.

When Mr Graham had re-established himself as a respectable person in old age he began to create a family for himself. He called the woman who had helped restore him (who was twenty years younger than he was) his mother, and once a week wrote a long letter to her, trying to maintain her concern. He also adopted a 'daughter', a young married woman with three small children whom he had met in a park. She became very fond of him, and her husband, too, took a great interest in the old man and liked to be treated as a son-in-law. Their three small children became grandchildren for him. But he also picked up a woman in a pub, whom he called his 'mistress', who had eight illegitimate children. He carried on a most exciting 'affair' with her for several years, with many ups and downs, and although there was obviously never a sexual relationship, it became the romance of Mr Graham's life, about which he wrote endlessly in his weekly letters to his 'mother'. It seems possible that in his mind this woman was connected with an earlier relationship that may have landed him in difficulties. But when he became really ill, it was to the 'daughter' that he turned for help and she cared for him when it became clear that he was dying.

In these fantasized relationships Mr Graham could combine his need for conventional respectability with that for a slightly delinquent dangerous relationship, but it seems that he was only able to find this solution for his loneliness once he had found a 'mother'.

In all these cases, the fantasies were an aid for survival and should be accepted as such. However, if fantasies are destructive and persecuting, help should be sought to enable the old person to understand and perhaps resolve the guilt and conflict which is at the root of them. Although there may have been some indication of stress in earlier life, it may only become threatening to mental health in old age when powers of control are diminished and illness, bereavement or fear of death reactivate unresolved conflicts. These may in fact have their roots in childhood, for example in the oedipal period. As I mentioned before, in the chapter dealing with loss, it was during the writing of *Death and the Family* that I became aware of how powerfully incestuous fantasies and the guilt which is so often attached to them are stirred up through death and the final separation.

The story of Mrs Miller illustrates this. As a child she had been her father's favourite and was determined that his position should be acknowledged by her older sister and as far as possible by her mother. The result was a very ambivalent relationship with both mother and sister.

When Mrs Miller grew into an attractive young woman she had many boyfriends and many proposals of marriage. However, none were accepted until she met a man whose job kept him frequently away from home for long spells and who allowed her to choose a house in the immediate neighbourhood of her parents. This enabled her to maintain the close relationship with her father. She had two daughters who she tried to keep as far away as possible from their grandfather (to whom she still needed to be the most important person) and from the girls' father. In spite of this, her younger daughter, Susan, became her father's darling, and a very close relationship developed between them. She, too, was a most attractive girl, but in contrast to her mother, Susan seemed to be aware of the inherent dangers in such closeness to the father. She married a foreigner who took her abroad. This did not improve the relationship between father and mother as each blamed the other for the loss of this daughter.

After the death of her husband Mrs Miller, then nearly eighty, became very angry and suspicious. Being estranged from her only sister and her two daughters, she felt that everybody was against her. Her paranoid distrust of all her female relatives turned into a general fear of persecution and eventually lead to a psychotic breakdown.

It seems to me that the disciplines most concerned with the mental health of old people often over-estimate organic factors and see disturbed behaviour as mainly caused by senile dementia, which is considered an irreversible and progressive destruction of the brain. Someone like Mrs Miller, however, can only be helped and understood by considering her case in relation to her life-story, and one can only hope that more and more psycho-therapeutically orientated work will be done with the old mentally disturbed.

There is of course irrefutable medical evidence to show that dementia, arising from the destruction of brain cells, does occur in old people. But by no means all is clear about the nature of this illness. Why, for example, does it occur in some people when still in their fifties and sixties, while others, apparently with a superabundance of brain cells, can continue to cope, despite organic alteration, into an extended old age without much mental or behavioural impairment. If changes in behaviour do occur, especially sudden changes, it is therefore important to look for other causes. These may be found in depression, which is treatable, or in a reaction to prescribed drugs or anaesthetics, or in various physical conditions such as disturbed thyroid functions, or a sudden onset of deafness or other physical disability. Bereavement or other significant losses or bewildering changes in environment may lead to confusion. Health visitors have told me that their old patients now often behave quite irrationally because they cannot understand the inflationary changes in money value and refuse to eat or keep their fires on, even if they actually have enough money to meet their bills.

When sudden changes of functioning take place, it is especially important to consider all the areas of a person's life. For one old woman it was a flood in her basement flat which she could not control that led to the onset of steadily growing confusion. She had always prided herself on being able to cope and throughout her life had avoided awareness of painful experiences. The loss of her beloved father and her brother in most alarming circumstances were never mentioned and had led to the utter denial of tragic events. But the flood, and her helplessness in the face of it, could not be denied, and to survive her defeat she withdrew into confusion.

Another striking example of flight into confusion is that of a seventy-year-old woman whose husband, a man of prominent position, had completely controlled her life and the running of the household. He insisted that he adored his charming wife: 'She can dance on my hands', he used to say, but it never occurred to him to include her in any decision taking. When he died suddenly she seemed completely unable to face up to and accept the fundamental changes which his death would make to her life. From the moment of his death she remained removed from reality. She showed no distress, nor ever mentioned his name, but smiling happily, talked only about fairies, princesses and other pleasant things. Her family felt that if she were made to accept her loss it would lead to a mental breakdown and so nobody made a serious attempt to destroy her illusions. Financially well provided for, she was able to stay in her usual surroundings, affectionately cared for until she died in her sleep a year later.

In considering how far old people who resist reality should be helped to face up to it, each individual case has to be dealt with differently. When my old friend who was driven into confusion by the flood in her flat tells me about her plans for a wonderful trip to Australia and the many important people who are waiting for her there, I do not attempt to undermine her belief in her story.

Recently, her sister, fifteen years younger than herself, died unexpectedly and when a relative attempted to break the sad news to her, my friend, usually a very poor sleeper, insisted on going to bed at midday and slept without moving for twenty-three hours. In spite of demonstrating in this way her resistance to take in the painful news, I insisted on repeating it to her until she was able to accept it. I did this because I felt that the continued denial of this sister's death, whose coming visit she had eagerly expected, could only increase her confusion. Events proved that once she was able to acknowledge that she had lost her sister, she began to make compensatory plans, such as trying to improve her position in the old people's home by taking on more responsibility. Although some of her actions in this direction were quite irrational, on the whole the acceptance of her loss helped her to settle better and led to more frequent spells of responding sensibly.

Such an improvement is remarkable in institutional care in which confusion and so-called senile dementia often seem to spread among the residents like an infection. Unfortunately the training of doctors and nurses often does not provide sufficient experience of the treatment of mental disorders of old people, and this may increase their ambivalent attitude towards the aged. As mentioned in Chapter Four, much of this ambivalence is often caused by the therapists' own conflicts and guilt about personal relationships with old parents and other elderly relatives, or by fear of their own old age and death. This creates a vicious circle of collusive interaction between the old and their helpers as each reinforce in the other what they most fear. And because there is a lack of appropriate community and out-patient services, many old people end up in mental hospitals, which is not where they ought to be.

However, I said earlier in this chapter that there is hope for a change as a broader-based training fosters new ideas among doctors, nurses and social workers, and provides geriatric work with an exciting challenge. One of the new methods which has proved helpful for very confused people who have hitherto been regarded as hopeless is reality orientation. This is being used in a variety of ways. The aim is always to increase the patient's ability to keep in touch with reality by the frequent repetition of simple factual information, as well as by avoiding changes in the environment. As far as possible, the same staff care for the same individual and always identify themselves and the resident by name.

I am not qualified to discuss this, or any other method of treatment, but I feel the need to emphasize once again that therapeutic effectiveness will always depend on the degree of individual care for, and personal contact with, the old person. The most immediate way to increase the mental health and happiness of an old person is to show genuine interest in his personality, his life, and his relationships. That this is beginning to be understood by the caring professions offers the best hope not only of making their work gratifying, but of promoting and improving the physical and mental health of our old population.

CHAPTER SEVEN

The search for a meaning

In this book so far I have tried to understand old people and to present their particular problems and concerns within the context of their life-situations and their relationships. Attempting now to move a little away from what might be called the horizontal line, we must keep in mind what we have learned as we consider the less tangible aspects of old age, such as doubts and beliefs about the meaning and purpose of life. In previous stages of the life-cycle these may not have varied much, but in old age, as death approaches, they must gain new momentum; then the question will inevitably be asked: 'Was my life worth living?'

To face this question it is vitally important that an old person is able to believe that the world is different because he or she has been in it. For every creature contributes at every moment of its existence to the continuous process of creation by reacting to whatever happens to it. The value of the contribution which we make may well be influenced by the degree of consciousness with which we make it.

Old age may impair the mental and physical faculties of a person, but it certainly increases the sum of his experiences. The privilege of age over youth lies in having had more opportunities to interpret experiences. These may strengthen the degree of consciousness with which his reactions are made and will thus make life more worth living as well as helping towards the acceptance of death. For the more fully we live our lives, the more ready we shall be for death.

In very old age, when mental and physical faculties have diminished, the stated readiness to die may be as well an expression of relief that at last the inescapable obligation to react to whatever happens can be ended. On the other hand, Lydia Maria Child in *Looking towards Sunset* says: 'After life has passed its maturity, great care should be taken not to become indifferent to the affairs of the world. It is salutary, both for the mind and the heart to take an interest in some of the great questions of the age . . . Nothing is more healthy for the soul than to go out of ourselves . . . We thus avoid brooding over our bodily pains, our mental deficiencies or our past moral shortcomings. We forget to notice whether others neglect us or not, whether their advantages are superior to ours or not . . . a continual preparation for eternal progress is the wisest and happiest way to live here.'*

I thought of this quotation when reading the letters written to Mary Spain by people aged eighty to one hundred in reply to a so far unpublished enquiry about their beliefs. Her enquiry, sent to three hundred men and women in that age group, was answered by two-thirds of them. Many of them replied very fully, all of them with serious consideration. Except for their age, the correspondents had nothing in common. They belonged to every conceivable religion and denomination, or to none at all, but whatever they believed was of ultimate concern to them. I was struck by the fact that in the more than one hundred contributions I read, only one person said: 'I am eighty-seven years old, my eyesight is poor, I find it difficult to concentrate and may not be able to do justice to your interesting enquiry.' Nobody else even mentioned an impediment of old age; they were all able 'to go out of themselves' for something that gave meaning to their lives.

A person who throughout his or her long life has been securely rooted in a religious belief can acquire great strength in old age. Catherine Booth, the ninety-three-years-old granddaughter of the founder of the Salvation Army, demonstrated this most strikingly when she spoke on television at Christmas 1979 about her life and her family. She had no doubts. Her religious tradition had formed her personality; her inner security made her speak without pretensions and with a great sense of humour. She did not need to cling to the safety of religious topics and watching her it was easy to understand how she had won at her old age the award of best after-dinner speaker of the year. She was as much at home in this world as in her expectations of a future one.

* Quoted by James Luther Adams in *Ageing: Theological Perspectives.*

Yet for many people belief in an afterlife may be frightening or distressing. One woman who had always been an agnostic, but a rather unsure and slightly guilty one, knew that she was dying of cancer. In her last days she suffered a stroke, and for a short period was unconscious. Afterwards she was radiant because, she said, 'I have already been on the other side, and now that I know with absolute certainty that there is no life after life I can die in peace.'

A clergyman had made his wife promise not to see him after his death as he felt that this would interfere with her belief in resurrection. Nevertheless, when he died his widow went against his wish and said good-bye to him in the hospital mortuary. Afterwards she told me: 'I am so thankful I went. He looked so young, so beautiful, and I felt with deepest gratitude: here lies the body of my lover.'

My own husband, who died a triumphant death, said on one of his last days, after we had looked together at some reproductions of Greek vases that depicted smiling farewells: 'They could smile, because sin had not been invented yet.'

As for myself, I can only reject a firm belief in an afterlife: how can we know? But I am quite prepared to let myself be surprised. People who talk with great certainty about their spiritual experiences are liable to interfere with such open expectations. On the other hand, I feel much in accord with the very old mother of a friend of mine who is, he told me, impatient to die and join her husband. She says: 'Your father will be standing there, looking at his watch and saying: "She was always unpunctual and now she is late again." '

This is familiar to me because I have also experienced feelings that arise from memories of a loved person which not only do not diminish after his death but seem to get stronger as time passes. These feelings of the presence of the dead person have for me nothing to do with spiritualism. They arise from the strength of the relationship during life. My concern is with the here and now, and with my contribution to the continuous process of creation which I mentioned earlier in this chapter. The eternal question, it seems to me is: how far do firm beliefs in God, the Creator, and in another world, help or hinder our own contribution on this earth?

C. G. Jung says in *Modern Man in Search of Soul*:* 'As a physician I am convinced that it is hygienic—if I may use the word—to discover in death a goal towards which to strive; and that shrinking away from it is something unhealthy and abnormal which robs the second half of life of its purpose. I therefore consider the religious teaching of life hereafter consonant with the life of psychic hygiene. When I live in a house which I know will fall about my head within the next two weeks, all my vital functions will be impaired by the thought; but if on the contrary I feel myself to be safe, I can dwell there in a normal and comfortable way. From the standpoint of psychotherapy it would therefore be desirable to think of death as only a transition—one part of a life-process whose extent and duration escape our knowledge.'

In Chapter Three I mentioned how delightful it is to meet a truly loving, very old couple, such as the Franks or the Jameses. Mr and Mrs Gould are another couple of this kind. They met as students at university and have been married for sixty-five years. He is ninety-two years old and she eighty-nine; they never talk about their approaching death, but give the impression of being at perfect ease about it. Mrs Gould's father was a presbyterian missionary but she herself has been an agnostic from early adulthood. Mr Gould, who came from a farming family, studied theology and became a methodist minister. As such he went to New Zealand but while he was there he left the church. In 1920 he obtained a job at the university in Vienna and there became deeply involved with the Student Christian Movement. He and his wife were overwhelmed by the poverty in Vienna, the many children with rickets, the students who could not work because they were too hungry. All their energies were spent in attempting to relieve the misery, and throughout their long lives this has remained their chief concern. Their commitment to academic teaching as well as to organized religion has been subordinated to

* Kegan Paul, London 1933, p. 129.

their concern for human beings. This indeed has become the basis of their lives. It has extinguished all religious and dogmatic differences: they no longer discriminate between the religious and the secular. The more human beings are seized by the sustaining and demanding sense of life, the less they are in need of a religious label.

Paul Tillich writes in *Morality and Beyond*:* 'The fundamental concept of religion is the state of being grasped by an ultimate concern, by an infinite interest, by something one takes unconditionally seriously!'

Derek who is nearly ninety years old feels himself to be a deeply religious man. He lives alone in an uncomfortable country cottage with a small chapel in which he says mass. He is a man of many gifts and considerable charm but leads a rather lonely and sad old age. He insists that his parents had not wanted him, and that he never felt securely loved by them. He longed to love them but was only able to show or feel affection for them when they were dying. As he felt he could not truly belong to them, he wanted to become separate from them, and attempted to achieve this through his choice of an artistic career, an area of activity that was alien to them; through his conversion to Roman Catholicism which they strongly opposed; and through his homosexual relationships. He remained, however, extremely attached to the house in which they lived. His lonely old age is spent in an inconvenient cottage close to it. Derek has been highly successful as an artist and a teacher of art. He is attractive to and attracted by many people, but he has never been able to commit himself fully to anybody or anything. His sexual as well as his intellectual, spiritual and religious passions have tossed him in several directions but failed to give him fulfilment. Having felt unloved, he could not truly love himself, and that means not being able truly to love others.

In later life Derek has several times been severely ill and near to death. Yet he has always 'miraculously' recovered. It does not seem too far from the truth to feel that it is because he has lacked the courage to be his true self, he cannot find the courage to die.

* *Religious Perspectives*, Vol. 9, Routledge & Kegan Paul, 1964.

Rosemary Gordon says: 'Those who are open both to the life forces and the death forces are people who can think and test and learn but who can also let go of these faculties without excessive pain or resentment.'*

This is probably the most difficult and demanding task of our lives and can only be achieved if not too many painful experiences have remained unresolved. How impending death and bereavement can stir up early childhood memories and repressed traumas is shown by the story of Michelangleo.† He was the second son of a father who was a minor customs official but so proud of his ancestry that he considered it below his dignity to work. His wife, also from a good family, was very delicate. When Michelangelo was born she was only twenty. She had a fall in the last stages of the pregnancy and this may have been the reason why the baby was given to a wet nurse, the daughter of a stonemason who lived a few miles outside Florence. Michelangelo stayed with the stonemason's family until he was ten years old and later used to say that it was no wonder that he had obtained so much gratification from the chisel as he drank it in with the mother's milk. His own parents had three more sons within the next five years. They visited him frequently, and each time it seems reasonable to imagine that he must have hoped that he would be allowed to join them. At some stage, too, he must have become aware of the wide social and material gulf between his foster parents and his natural family.

When Michelangelo was six years old his mother died. His father remarried when the boy was ten, and only then was he allowed to join his family again. It may be that the frustrations of Michelangelo's early life can be seen in his inclination to fly into rages, especially when provoked. He was also insecure in his sexual relationships, more attracted to men than to women; and the memory of his poor upbringing seems to have been expressed

* Rosemary Gordon, 'Dying and Creating: A search for meaning', *Journal of Analytical Psychology*, Vol. 4, published by the Society of Analytical Psychology.

† Andrew Peto, 'The Rondanini Pieta, Michelangelo's Infantile Neurosis', *International Review of Psychoanalysis* 1979, No. 6, 183.

in an exaggerated way in his personal manners; for example he did not like to change his stockings until they had literally to be torn off his feet, taking some of the skin with them. On the other hand, he highly valued his connections with the papal court and with the high aristocracy and enjoyed for long spells the patronage of both.

In 1555, when Michelangelo was eighty years old, Urbino, his servant and devoted caretaker for many years, was dying. He had persistently urged Michelangelo to finish the Florentine Pieta on which he had been working for several years. This sculpture must have been of special importance to Michelangelo as he had asked that it should be used for his own tomb and one of the four figures, Nicodemus, is a self-portrait. A few days before Urbino's death Michelangelo flew into a rage and destroyed the leg of Jesus. It was later reconstructed by someone else but never to Michelangelo's satisfaction. Soon after Urbino's death Michelangelo started the Rondanini Pieta. The figures of the mother and son are standing close together and the heads look very much alike; from the side they seem to be one person. This Pieta has been regarded by several of Michelangelo's biographers as his attempt at reconciliation with his mother. He never completely finished it, but was still working on it a few days before his death, at the age of eighty-nine.

Michelangelo's seemingly irrational response to Urbino's death can probably be understood as a reactivation of his pain and repressed fury when as a child he felt rejected by his mother. That he attempted in the Rondanini Pieta a reconciliation with his mother may indicate that on some level he was aware of the connection between the loss of Urbino and the loss of his mother.

By the time they reach their mid-seventies most people have experienced the deaths of friends, relatives and neighbours and have become more familiar with loss through death. In how far this helps them to accept the death of a person very close to them or to contemplate their own death will largely depend on the inner and outer circumstances of their lives.

Belief in an afterlife and reunion with those already in the other world naturally affects attitudes to death and bereavement.

But the ever-growing number of organizations offering help to the bereaved, of which only a few are connected with the churches, indicates the need of more and more bereaved people for support and counsel in the here and now. The services of the Cruse clubs who give help of this kind to widows and widowers are constantly being extended, so that there are now seventy branches in Great Britain; and a growing number of social service departments are setting up their own projects to help the bereaved.

It has been noted, however, that only a very small percentage of those asking for help are from among the very old. This may be because for them it is becoming more difficult to take steps to get help. Or it may indicate that the very old accept bereavement as a natural event which they have to endure without expecting any help. GPs with whom I have discussed this question have expressed surprise that relatively very few of their oldest patients ask for help after a bereavement, in contrast to their younger patients.

A research project conducted at Keele University into the responses to bereavement of the very old found some evidence that feelings of loss and bereavement are different in quite a marked degree in this age group from that of others. The characteristic feeling of grief appears to be less intense. The study distinguishes between inhibited grief in which responses which appear to be subdued may well be associated with physical and psychological symptoms, possibly leading to mental illness and suicide; and chronic grief and intense feelings over a longer time than is found in typical grief, perhaps giving rise to hostility, suspicion and apathy.

Because of these apparently different responses, Dr Colin Parkes has excluded widows over sixty-five from his studies. He strongly supports the general feeling that much too little is known about the very old, and emphasizes the need for further studies to help us to understand better the varied responses to bereavement of very old people.

The examples in this chapter will make it clear that my contribution is far removed from research. They are drawn from my experiences as a social worker and psychotherapist, as well as from stories told to me by friends and colleagues. They have—however—confirmed most strikingly the tremendous variations that we can observe in the responses of old people to death and bereavement.

The one exception is probably the death of an adult son or daughter, especially one who has been the practical and moral support of old parents. This loss is usually felt as a shattering blow from which very old people may never recover.

Responses to the loss of a marriage partner will largely depend on the nature of the marriage relationship and the milieu in which the couple lived. If they were still living in their own home, the survivor may be compelled to give it up, suffering thereby a multiple loss. Such an upheaval at a time of grief may have great effects on mental and physical health.

On the other hand, it may happen that even a very old widow who has nursed an ailing husband for many years may gain a new lease of life after his death. I know of an eighty-seven-year-old woman who became visibly rejuvenated after the death of her demanding husband. She now has a number of 'boyfriends' ('I believe in safety in numbers') and whenever I meet her she mentions with pride how much her neighbours and friends at church admire her 'fortitude' in her bereavement.

Another woman I know lost her husband after sixty-five years of a very united marriage. Yet she continues to live with him, talks about 'we' and 'ours', and fills her life with all that had been their mutual concern. Everything she does is so closely linked with her husband that she does not mourn his loss in the usual way. She is a deeply religious and highly cultured woman, and while she is not longing to die, she is living in preparation for it.

Both these women had no children. Another widow of the same age had a son and a daughter, both married, and several grandchildren. She was always ailing, and nobody had imagined that her husband, who was five years younger and always fit, would die before her. He was a highly respected member of his community, deeply involved with social concerns. He died at home after a short illness, surrounded by his family, a conscious and peaceful death. His widow found it difficult to grasp the fact of his death, but the loving care of her family, and the concern of her neighbours and the community, have helped her to make a new life of her own. While she deeply misses her husband, she admits reluctantly that her life has become enriched in many ways, and her health has improved, even though she is approaching the age of ninety.

All these old widows have been able to continue to live in their homes, and have not been seriously disabled. Nevertheless, their varied responses to the loss of their husbands show how impossible it is to generalize about mourning in old age.

The death of a partner in a homosexual relationship may be especially painful, because the surviving partner has no family to support him, the community does not acknowledge him as a mourner, and the family of the lost lover may be hostile, making difficulties about arrangements for and participation in the funeral. I have heard of a lover's deep distress because his flowers had been removed from the coffin. Other sorts of hurtful things may be done, more often perhaps out of thoughtlessness than resentment. If the lover has died intestate, it will be difficult for the partner to make a claim on the estate, and he or she may even be left without a home.

Information is lacking about the effect of a lover's death on the homosexual survivor. I happen to have personal knowledge of two men, neighbours of mine, who had lived together all their adult lives in a quiet, unobtrusive homosexual relationship. They were both in their late seventies when one of them became ill and was devotedly nursed by the other. After his death the lover carefully arranged all that was necessary, and died ten days later, apparently of natural causes.

Survivors' responses will also depend on the process of dying. This can be greatly affected by the atmosphere around the deathbed which can help or hinder a relaxed death. Quite often those closest to the patient undermine his courage to die because they show so clearly that they cannot bear to face their own loss.

A woman doctor, in hospital during the last phase of inoperable cancer, was being kept alive by every means of intensive treatment. When her brother, himself a doctor, came to visit her from abroad, he was horrified by the extent of her suffering. 'Why ever do you allow this to go on, when it's so entirely against your principles?' he asked. Her answer was: 'My daughters won't let me die.' After the brother had helped the daughters, both qualified doctors, to see that they had allowed their commitment to medical science to stand in the way of loving common sense, and thus caused their mother much pain and distress, they arranged for their mother's discharge from hospital, and after a few days she died peacefully and gratefully at home.

The Hospice Movement has developed methods of sensitive care of the dying. There are now about fifty hospices in Great Britain and the basic ideas of hospice care are beginning to infiltrate into general hospitals and especially into the terminal wards. The senior social worker of a local geriatric hospital who has always taken a compassionate interest in her patients told me about a moving experience she has had. One of her patients was dying and during a spell of unconsciousness was wheeled into a side ward. When she returned to consciousness, she asked for every member of the staff and all those patients she had known well to come and say goodbye to her. She lovingly shook hands with each one of them, thanked them for all they had done for her, and expressed her good wishes for them and their families. Soon afterwards she went to sleep never to wake again. Everybody in the ward was deeply moved, and the staff was most impressed by the relief, the joy almost, with which their old patients, many of whom were likely to die soon, experienced death—as an occasion for celebration rather than a hidden, frightening event.

A friend of mine told me about her father's death in hospital. After a massive stroke he had developed pneumonia. The consultant took great care to explain to the family that he could be treated with drugs but that the extent of haemorrhage was so great that his chances of any kind of mental recovery were practically nil. It would therefore be better to let the pneumonia kill him. Although my friend's mother was a trained nurse and has always strongly resisted the idea of prolonged survival, at this moment her fear of losing her husband was such that she only reluctantly accepted the consultant's view. Once a decision to let him die had been made, every effort was made by the hospital to allow his death to be as peaceful as possible.

His family, and this meant up to ten people and a small baby, were encouraged to be with him any time of the day or night. The patient was a clergyman and he was able to receive (and appeared aware of doing so) the last rites of the church from his bishop, a close friend. My friend was particularly impressed by how much the nurses, who had seen her father only as a patient, seemed moved and distressed by his death. They made her feel that for them each death is a unique event.

In spite of these examples of relaxed deaths in hospital an increasing number of patients express the wish to die in their own homes. The staff of hospices have developed a domiciliary service giving full support both to the patient and to the family. And an increasing number of health authorities are also acknowledging the wish of patients to die at home by providing services to make this possible. Indeed, the present financial crisis in the health service supports such money-saving arrangements.

Personally, I am deeply grateful that all my dear ones have died at home quietly and relaxedly. The wish to do so, and the fear that the process of dying may be interfered with in hospital, is expressed in the great increase in the membership of Exit, the voluntary euthanasia society that believes in the right to die with dignity. The largest percentage of their members are middle-aged people who often join after they have watched the painful, lingering deaths of their parents or close relatives.

Although my stories indicate that it is just as impossible to generalize about the responses of very old people to death and bereavement as about those of other age groups, it is probably true that in very old age death has become more acceptable. This was confirmed to me by my aunt Flora who was nearly one hundred years old when a dearly loved friend of ours, a beautiful, much younger actess, died in an accident. I dreaded breaking the news to Flora and asked the matron of the home in which she lived whether it was advisable to do so. She reassured me, saying that such old people have got used to accepting death. And indeed, Flora took the news very calmly, and after asking a few relevant question turned to other concerns.

Flora was a remarkable person who had survived concentration camp, where she had cared for the blind, and many traumatic losses without losing her zest and love for life. Shortly before her hundredth birthday, I wanted to give her a special treat by taking her out to lunch at her favourite restaurant, which was only a few yards away from the home. She was still very interested in her appearance and dressed up carefully for this outing, but a few steps from the restaurant she fell and rolled into the gutter. Alarmed passers-by stopped to help me lift up the dishevelled Flora and carry her back to the home. But she was determined not to miss her special lunch. Straightening herself up energetically, and having restored her appearance, she went on and thoroughly enjoyed a three-course dinner.

All family members of the younger generation adored Flora; her unquenchable love of life and love for people was infectious. Actually, she did not live to celebrate her hundredth birthday. A few days before one of her favourite nephews, a doctor, came to visit her from the USA. He brought with him a five-pound box of cherry-brandy chocolates which had been presented to him by Nestlés, of which he was a board member. Flora had always adored these chocolates and he started feeding her with them. Both of them greatly enjoyed their 'sweet' reunion, but in the following night Flora became sick and died. This caused great upset in the home where elaborate preparations had been made for the birthday celebrations, but I could not mourn her death. I felt that it would have been her choice to die after such a happy day.

To write this book has been a great experience for me, an eighty-three-year-old. Many of the things which I have learned about my contemporaries have come as a surprise, especially the tremendous variations in feelings about doubts and beliefs, death and bereavement. I feel that everything that concerns the emotional life of the very old has so far been sadly neglected or misunderstood. This very personal book cannot provide any answers, but perhaps it will encourage better qualified people to search further into ways that increase the understanding and self-confidence of the very old so that they can contribute their abilities and talents more fully to their communities and have a happier life.

I began the first chapter on a very personal note and can end my contribution only in an almost equally personal way. Recently a fourteen-year-old relative asked me: 'Aren't you afraid to die?'

'Not as far as I know,' I answered. 'I am almost looking forward to it.'

The boy was puzzled, and the more I thought about my reply, the more puzzled I became too. Can it really be true that I am looking forward to die? I still enjoy my life and live it as fully as my diminishing physical resources allow. If I think about death, it is with the hope that I will still be truly alive when it comes. To be aware of death makes life more precious and asking questions about the meaning of life more urgent.

C. G. Jung wrote when he was eighty-six:*'In spite of all uncertainties, I feel a solidity underlying all existence and a continuity in my mode of being.

'The world into which we are born is brutal and cruel, and at the same time of divine beauty. Which element we think outweighs the other, whether meaninglessness or meaning, is a matter of temperament. Probably, as in all metaphysical questions, both are true: life is—or has—meaning and meaninglessness. I cherish the anxious hope, that meaning will preponderate and win the battle.'

***Memoirs, Dreams and Reflections*, Collins and Routledge & Kegan Paul, 1963.

CHAPTER EIGHT

Retirement

by ALEDA ERSKINE

The Challenge of a Long Life *originated in my reflections on my own experience of old age—I was eighty-two when I started to write it. Perhaps for personal reasons, it was this age group which gained my greatest interest. Yet I was well aware that the way an individual copes with the retirement years has an enormous influence on the experience of later old age. As I thought more deeply about this question, however, I realized that I would not be able to do justice to it myself and so, as I have explained in the Foreword, I asked Aleda Erskine if she would tackle the all-important theme of retirement.*

Aleda seemed to me just the right person to write the chapter since she had already studied and written about retirement during her work as education officer with 'Help the Aged'. We discussed her contribution fully together, and talked through the other themes in the book, reaching a common understanding of the most important issues of old age. The fight against the segregation of the old is a major message of the book, and the co-operation with Aleda, who was born in 1948, has thus been for me an expression of one of my strongest beliefs: the continuing need for young and old to work together and to be prepared to learn from each other.

LILY PINCUS

'Retirement'* should be about the possibility of new beginnings. And it seems fitting that such a passionately positive book about later life should end on a note of beginnings.

Lily Pincus asked me to write this last chapter because—although she was aware that for many people retirement had a profound effect on the rest of their lives—she had no real

* The word is full of defeatist overtones and, since it seems unavoidable, should be in quotation marks throughout. But they look unwieldy and are henceforth left out.

experience of it herself. Three days precisely, as recounted in Chapter One. I was reminded of Alex Comfort's* pronouncement that the ideal length of retirement is approximately two weeks.

To begin a new, highly creative career after retiring at seventy-five will probably never be a possibility for many people. (Though I think it should be an option for more.) But to *live* creatively in retirement, continuing to develop and use your talents and capacity for relationships, should be open to all who desire it. The reality is that for too many people retirement signifies the closing of doors rather than the entry into a new phase of life. So, the question I try to answer in this chapter echoes the question about later age in general that Lily Pincus sets herself in the Foreword: why do some people thrive during the early retirement years, while others merely survive?

RETIREMENT: A PSYCHO-SOCIAL TRANSITION

Although we often talk about retirement as a crisis or time of stress, to define it as such may be prejudging the issue. The psychiatrist Colin Murray Parkes has used a more neutral term, 'psycho-social transition',† to describe retirement and any major period of change which forces a person to restructure his/her ways of looking at the world and plans for living in it. This process always takes effort. The external change amounts to a radical change in the individual's 'life space'—that world of home, workplace, material possessions and relationships which we call our own. In turn, change is necessitated in all the assumptions we make about our 'life space': that 'assumptive world' which includes our way of life, sense of identity, knowledge and expectations about the future. To this 'assumptive world' we are tied with strong bonds because anything which can be called 'mine' (my job, my workmates, my home etc.) becomes part of myself. So, not surprisingly, there is usually strong resistance to

* A. Comfort, *A Good Age*, Mitchell Beazley, 1977.

† C. Murray Parkes, 'Psycho-social Transitions: A Field for Study', *Social Science and Medicine*, 1971.

change whenever that change requires us to give up a part of our 'life space' and therefore alter our 'assumptive world'. Hence the effort involved in facing a 'psycho-social transition' such as retirement. According to Colin Murray Parkes, when the transition is seen as total loss—whether or not that change involves a person or possession—the individual reaction will take the form of grief or mourning.

To see retirement, the ending of employment, as a psycho-social transition is to begin to explain the complex reactions it can provoke. Here is just one reaction, from a former senior consultant, quoted by Ronald Blythe in *The View in Winter*: 'I was depressed at the thought of retiring because I wasn't quite sure what would happen to me. You see, I had had my position for so long—my specialist work, my hospital, my staff, my professional travels, my teaching. All these things which I had were what I *was*, and to have to give them up at sixty-five left me with something quite unrecognisable. Old age for me has been the recognition of what was left when all that I was was taken away from me . . . '

The consultant's acute sense of bereavement is probably shared by only a minority of retirees. But difficulties in facing up to retirement are commonplace. A recent survey* showed that one-third of men and women coming up to retirement thought they would find it difficult to settle down. One quarter anticipated particular problems, mainly financial but also boredom or loneliness. Nearly half had mixed feelings about retirement while one half of men but only—interestingly—one quarter of women were positively looking forward to it.

The same survey asked a sample of men and women who had left work just over a year if they had 'settled down'. The majority, 77 per cent of men and 81 per cent of women felt they had, but a not insignificant minority—17 per cent of men and 12 per cent of women—said not. An earlier survey† found that although about one-half of retirees were quite happy and felt busy, about one-quarter felt time hang heavily. And for a very small number of

* S. Parker, *Older workers and Retirement*, OPCS, 1980.

† *The Attitudes of the Retired and Elderly*, Age Concern, 1974.

retirees, there is a little, controversial evidence to suggest that disenchantment with retirement may even be linked to death.

One more statistic to reckon with is the finding* that by far the most contented group of older people are the elderly workers.

THE CHANGES RETIREMENT BRINGS

Retirement brings choice and therefore uncertainty. What you retire from—your job, your workplace—is concrete; what you retire to—the activities, the relationships you enter into—are likely to be unplanned or unsure. This uncertainty, linked to the effects of change, is likely to provoke anxiety. Part of it is inevitable: it is the 'flip side' of the most positive aspect of retirement, the freedom to create your own life-style, to carve out your own role. But part of it is potentially destructive and avoidable. It is the uncertainty which is rooted in the general social ambivalence towards retirement as an institution: our doubt as to whether retirement is the beginning of a new chapter or in fact the end of the story.

Ever since its introduction in this country in the early years of the century, the image of retirement as fostered by governments and experts has fluctuated. For example, as recently as the early sixties the Government produced a leaflet on retirement which urged people to stay at work, saying that their knowledge, skill and experience should not be wasted and that in this way continued interest and companionship would be assured them: 'If you stay at work you will help to maintain prosperity as a nation.' But now the message has changed. The Government is backing early retirement schemes and sociologists and psychologists have stopped talking darkly about the perils of the 'roleless role' of retirement. There is a new, more positive view of retirement as a release from the forty-hour week and an opportunity to take up or extend activities in the social, cultural and political spheres.

* *The Elderly at Home*, OPCS, 1978.

It may have been no coincidence that this new vision of retirement emerged as unemployment became a problem after the post-war boom years. Chris Phillipson* has argued that governments—and academic opinion with them—have changed their minds about retirement in line with the fluctuation of the labour market. He maintains that it has been extremely useful to keep older people as a reserve pool of labour, to be used in periods of labour shortage or withdrawn in periods of slump.

Linked to this continued policy debate about the value of retirement to the country and to the individual has been the persistent failure of governments to create the kind of material infrastructure which would give the retired security and independence. One reason for this is that politically the retired are weak, with no organization tough enough to fight for the services and pensions which would enable all of their number to share in the 'good life'.

Another potent source of anxiety about retirement is the fear of ageing. Retirement is still often seen as the *rite-de-passage* to old age and the dominant image of the 'pensioner' in our society is an unglamorous one of an individual in physical and mental decline, the object—never the initiator—of policies and activities, Society is ageist. Compulsory retirement itself can be seen as a discriminatory practice based solely on age; and there are all sorts of subtler ways in which older people are treated as less than fully human on account of the number of their birthdays.

For women, retirement—either their own or, vicariously, their husband's—may intensify a fear of ageing which Susan Sontag suggests, in a famous essay,† may be more acute than a man's. There is, she writes, a 'double standard of ageing'. 'Society is much more permissive about ageing in men, as it is more tolerant of the sexual infidelities of husbands. Men are "allowed" to age, without penalty, in several ways that women are not . . . For most women, ageing means a humiliating process of gradual

* C. Phillipson, *The Emergence of Retirement*, Dept. of Sociology and Social Administration, University of Durham, 1978.

† S. Sontag, 'The Double Standard of Ageing', in V. Carver and P. Liddiard (Eds.), *An Ageing Population*, Hodder and Stoughton, 1978.

sexual disqualification. Since women are considered maximally eligible in early youth, after which their sexual value drops steadily, even young women feel themselves in a desperate race against the calendar.'

Fear of ageing by both men and women is intensified at retirement because of the vacuum of ideas about what retirement is *for*. So much of the rhetoric about retirement has a hollow ring because it is couched in negative terms: the 'freedom' is freedom from work, freedom from the clock, freedom from the boss. The 'opportunities' are often only opportunities to kill time when there is nothing useful to do.

We do not know what retirement is for because we have little idea what life is about apart from amassing money and goods and we are very confused about the place of work in human life. Here are three confusions:

We mistakenly identify gainful employment with work so that any non-gainful employment is devalued.

We do not see that alienation from certain processes of production is a response to the *organization of work*, not to work as such nor even to employment as such*.

We talk about the decline of the protestant work ethic—the idea that work is a means of earning a place in heaven—but we fail to recognize an older work ethic going back to Plato and to the Old Testament which values work as the expression of our creativity and brotherhood.

In his book, *Good Work*,† the economist E. F. Schumacher urged a return to this older ethic. The Cartesian revolution, he argues, has landed us in a metaphysical flatland where materialistic science is our only guide and the spiritual 'vertical dimension' has been removed from our map of knowledge: 'Science provides excellent guidance: it can do everything except lead us out of the dark wood of a meaningless, purposeless,

* For a discussion, see M. Jahoda, 'The psychological meanings of unemployment', *New Society*, 6 September, 1979.

† E. F. Schumacher, *Good Work*, Jonathan Cape, 1979.

"accidental" existence. Modern science answers the question What is Man? with such inspiring phrases as "a cosmic accident" or . . . "a naked ape".'

Schumacher argues that we should restore the 'vertical dimension' to life by returning to the traditional wisdom: that the purpose of each man's being is a journey of liberation from self towards perfection:

'To perfect himself, [man] needs purposeful activity in accordance with the injunction: "Whichever gift each of you have received, use it in service to one another, like good stewards dispensing the grace of God in its varied forms." From this, we may derive the three purposes of human work as follows:

'First, to provide necessary and useful goods and services.

'Second, to enable every one of us to use and thereby perfect our gifts like good stewards.

'Third, to do so in service to, and in co-operation with, others so as to liberate ourselves from inborn egocentricity.

'This threefold function makes work so central to human life that it is truly impossible to conceive of life at the human level without work . . . '

It also follows, of course, that work which does not encompass these three functions—which is not 'good work'—stands condemned. And Schumacher is a passionate critic of the world of work within our industrial system which he has described as 'mechanical, artificial, divorced from nature, utilizing only the smallest part of man's potential capabilities . . . (providing) no stimulus to self-perfection.' Within this system, most work is given only a utilitarian value: 'work is *nothing but* a more or less unpleasant necessity, and the less there is of it the better.'

If these ideas are accepted, then there are important consequences for our view of retirement.

Schumacher, I think, would have agreed with Alex Comfort's comment about the ideal length of time to retire. Certainly, the idea of retirement as having value chiefly as respite from work—a 'perpetual holiday' in the words of the brochure of one well-established pre-retirement course—is antithetical to these ideas of the centrality of work. The fact of having retired from gainful employment is irrelevant to the continued human need to use and develop our potentialities and serve other people.

The fact is, of course, that a man or woman's job may have had little to do with 'good work'. All the more need, therefore, for pre-retirement education, the adult educational opportunities and opportunities to participate fully in community life which would make it possible for the retiree to begin to realize his/her talents in retirement. In the main, as I shall point out, these are lacking.

'Good work' is not to be confused with mere activity. The experts who press the retired to keep active, take up exercise or voluntary work or hobbies in order to ward off the dangers of the rocking-chair have missed the point. So have the well-meaning charities who set up sheltered workshops for the retired in which the members work away at unskilled, mindless, light industrial tasks for a pittance. 'Good work' is not therapy (though it may be therapeutic)—as far as possible it is self-fulfilment.

It also follows that any policy or institution which makes it harder for the retired to live as neighbours with others, to co-operate or to serve them is suspect. In the UK we 'wall in' older people in all sorts of ways: for example, by failing to provide the domiciliary services which would keep them in the community and out of old people's homes and by keeping down pension levels.

I want to turn now from a discussion of the institution of retirement to focus in greater detail on the changes it brings to the life-style.

1. Loss of occupation Work may be boring or unpleasant for many people, but there is no sign that the motivation to work has gone out of fashion. In 1978 a National Opinion Poll survey of employed people in Britain found that a majority would not give up their job even if they could do so without loss of pay. The proportion rose to an astonishing 82 per cent for people just at retirement age.

What is it, then, that keeps us hooked to the daily round until many of us are forced to give up by an arbitrary age limit? The psychologist, Marie Jahoda, in a paper* on the psychology of unemployment, says that 'there are latent consequences of employment as a social institution which meet human needs of an enduring kind.' These 'latent consequences' have immensely important psychological implications, summed up in Freud's saying that work is man's strongest tie to reality.

First and foremost there is the time structure employment imposes on the waking day. This ties us to the 'here-and-now'. It prevents us from being swamped by the past, or by dreams of the future. We often resent the imposed time structure. But remove it and you get the burdensome time experience of the unemployed. Or of many retired people. As Marie Jahoda writes, 'a major ingredient in the psychological burden of retirement is the absence of "regular hours".'

Secondly, 'employment implies regularly shared experiences and contacts with people outside the family.'

Thirdly, employment 'links an individual to goals and purposes which transcend his own'. She comments: 'work makes inescapable the realisation that no man is an island unto himself . . . take away this daily experience that efforts must be combined, and the unemployed (or the unhappily retired) are left with a sense of uselessness, a sense of being on the scrap heap.'

Fourthly, 'employment defines aspects of status and identity.'

Finally, 'employment enforces activity . . . presents an opportunity for actions whose consequences are visible, for the daily exercise of competence and skill.'

The major task at retirement is to find new ways to meet these psychological needs. One indication of how hard this is to do is the statistic quoted earlier: that, on the whole, the older worker is more content than his/her retired neighbour.

Three chapters could be written about the need for pre-retirement education, imaginative community work openings and attractive adult educational opportunities for the retired. Here, I can only say that although there are, scattered up and down the country, excellent projects—a very great deal more

*Jahoda, Op. cit.

needs to be done to draw retired people from manual and semi-skilled occupational backgrounds into these activities. Just to take the adult education field: at present, a tiny two per cent of retired people participate. Yet, as Dr Mark Abram* has said, 'all those non-monetary satisfactions found in the work situation are equally available to those who study in post-retirement education classes.' What stops them? First, a lack of motivation, mainly because the majority of the retired have had no brush with education since leaving school. And secondly, the lack of special educational programmes to promote attendance among older people. As I write, there seems little prospect of an expanded take-up of education by the retired. The UK adult education service is being savagely slashed and in many areas, fees have been raised beyond the price that most pensioners can afford.

If most or all of the psychological needs met—to some extent—by paid work go unfulfilled in retirement, then the experience of retirement can feel similar to the depressed reactions to long-term unemployment described by Marie Jahoda. Or, in Colin Murray Parkes's term, a grief reaction sets in as a response to a psychosocial transition perceived as loss. This grief reaction has four phases: a phase of numbness, a phase of active searching to replace or find the lost object or person, a phase of depression and finally—though not always—a phase of reorganization when new plans, new ways of coping and new assumptions about the self are built up.

2\. *Loss of income* Most people halve their income on retirement and also join the ranks of one of the poorest groups in society. To take some figures: the 1978 Report of the Diamond Commission showed that—taking the poverty line as 120 per cent of Supplementary Benefit level—over half the retired are poor. Over a quarter of pensioners—about 2½ million—need to claim Supplementary Benefit and another half million entitled to claim fail to do so.

* Mark Abram, 'Education and the Elderly', Alice Foley Annual Memorial Lecture WEA Bolton, February 1980.

Among pensioners as a group, however, there are big differences in income. There is an economic sexual 'double standard of ageing' with the single woman particularly disadvantaged. Income levels also tend to drop with advanced age.

Living at or around the poverty line imposes very real constraints on the individual life-style. It is not just a question of cutting back on consumer goods; social life is restricted because entertaining and visits to the pub are curtailed; holidays and cultural activities such as film and theatre trips all become impossibilities or rare luxuries.

How important a factor is income drop in determining adjustment to retirement?

The first point is a general one: so long as we, as a society, fail to assure the retired of an income which enables them to participate fully in the common culture, the stigma attached to the 'pensioner' status will not be eradicated. On an individual level, a recent report* had this to say: 'The elderly with lower incomes appeared to suffer more ill-health and to be less able to enjoy the positive aspects of life than those with higher incomes.'

Whether or not many individual retired people on lower incomes consciously resent their scarce resources is another matter. Dissatisfaction over money depends on your subjective evaluation of the gap between your goals and the financial resources at hand. But the majority of people coming up to retirement do not work out precise goals for their retirement; either they do not dream at retirement or they modify their dreams and goals to suit their reduced circumstances. Thus one survey† found that, when asked what they disliked about retirement, very few retired people mentioned financial difficulty; yet when asked for suggestions to help elderly people, financial suggestions predominated.

3. Changing social relationships Even when relationships with colleagues are superficial, they fulfil important psychological needs. As Marie Jahoda writes: 'Shared experience with others

* Royal Commission on Distribution of Income, 1978.
† Op. cit., OPCS, 1978.

outside the family ties you to social reality. It . . . gives access to a wider pool of experience than would otherwise be possible.'

For many people relationships at work allow the expression of a side of their personalities which is otherwise restrained. There is for example the office 'joker' who may be given few opportunities at home to be a clown. There is the foreman who enjoys laying down the law at work and then returns to an overbearing wife at home.

Replacing the companionship at work is particularly necessary and particularly hard for the unmarried, the widowed and the growing numbers of older divorced people. Society is not kind to the single. If a retiree has been recently widowed the stress of adjusting to these two events can be enormous. The social skills involved in making new friends let alone beginning a new courtship—are considerable. It can be very hard to learn or resurrect them in your sixties.

For the married retiree who finds it hard to make new social contacts, an additional strain is going to bear on the marriage. But in any case, the retirement of either partner or both imposes two major changes on the marriage: the need to renegotiate the household division of labour and the need to find a new balance between time shared and time alone, between dependence and interdependence.

The effect of the women's movement on the older woman is difficult to estimate. My impression—and there is evidence to back it up*—is that there is far greater reluctance on the part of women to throw up their own lives to take care of their husbands in retirement. This reluctance, together with the often difficult lot of the single woman in retirement, may explain why women on the whole are less inclined to look forward to retirement than men. Different expectations of retirement on the part of husband and wife can lead to a serious mismatch of retirement goals. The husband, for example, may put pressure on a working wife to give up her job at his retirement. A woman who has put together a new life for herself after her children have left home may resent

* See, for example, D. Jacobson, *Attitudes Towards Work and Retirement in Three Firms*, Unpublished Ph D Thesis, LSE, 1970.

the upset to her routine that the continued presence of her husband entails.

If the marriage has kept channels of communication open and if husband and wife have previously struck a balance between individual and joint friends and activities, then a couple will not find it hard to adapt to retirement. In fact, for some couples retirement sparks a new warmth and tenderness in the relationship. But for others, work may have masked sexual or emotional incompatibilities in the marriage which then become inescapable in retirement. Old conflicts may need resolution and, to do this, new channels of communication must be found.

RETIREMENT: LOSS OR GAIN?

I want to go back to my first question: what is it that determines whether retirement is a turning-point for the better or for the worse?

One obvious consideration is health. Clearly, it will influence the enjoyment of retirement, but is it of overriding importance? Experts disagree. One recent writer* has gone so far as to suggest that there are two kinds of retirement—one for the really healthy minority and another (much gloomier) variety for the unhealthy. Others maintain, as Lily Pincus does, that many people can overcome quite severe health handicaps and still live full lives. Almost certainly the incidence of ill health in later life has been exaggerated. In a Government survey carried out in 1976, 2,600 people aged sixty-five or more were asked: 'Would you say in general you enjoy good health or not?' Over three-quarters (78 per cent) answered 'Yes'. Only among the over eighty-fives did the negative rate rise to 40 per cent; among those of retirement age, the negative responses were less than 20 per cent.

On the psychological level, Colin Murray Parkes† provides a tentative answer to my question: 'Whether the situation (a psycho-social transition) is seen as gain or loss, one is tempted to

* John Nicholson, *Seven Ages*, Fontana Paperback, 1980.
† Op. cit.

think that the crucial factor may be the way in which the individual copes with the process of change.' It is an answer which is reaffirmed and developed in this book. One constant theme has been that the way we cope with change and loss of all kinds at all stages of life determines our capacity to grow. Implicit in this theme has been a need to understand an individual's life history before reaching an understanding of that individual in later life.* Yet, however important the individual's physical material and personal resources at the point of retirement, it is still essential to look at the range of choices offered to the retiree by society as a whole, by the retiree's occupational background and local community. Only by doing so can we understand the complicated interaction between the individual and the social environment which determines the outcome of the experience of retirement.

A key factor is the individual's experience of work up to retirement: more particularly the extent to which the job allowed 'work' and 'life' to converge and enrich each other and the extent to which the job allowed a comparable standard of living to be carried over into retirement. Chris Phillipson has argued this idea:† 'We know that for many workers their occupational lives are a burden and a "cost". We assume, however, that much of this is erased when work finishes . . . I would like to reverse this argument and suggest that the real cost of work may only appear as the worker retires, and when he examines the resources available to him/her for the next 15 or 20 years. On the other hand, for the more fortunate whose work has allowed them to develop many levels of ability, the true benefit of their jobs may not be perceived until retirement. For these groups their work represents a past which can be used creatively within retirement. For others, however, where work has been a source of alienation, the "past" may be damaging, may even be a

* See also Malcolm Johnson, 'That Was Your Life: a biographical approach to later life' in V. Carver and P. Liddiard (Eds.), *An Ageing Population*, Hodder and Stoughton, 1981.

† C. Phillipson, 'The Sociology of the Transition', *Concord, Journal of the British Association for Service to the Elderly*, No. 17, pp. 13–19, May 1980.

threat to the individual's integrity and self-esteem. Certainly it can rarely be used in any useful way to develop an identity for retirement.'

To illustrate these points, Chris Phillipson contrasts a group of twenty-five car workers with a group of twenty-five architects—all men he had interviewed in depth. In comparison with the architects, all the car workers took a steep drop in income on retirement and had to lower their standard of living in line with this. There were also big differences in the work/life 'fit' for the two groups. The architects had acquired manual, intellectual and social skills during their careers: engineering, painting, carpentry, modelling, writing, mixing with all degrees of people—all skills which could be transferred and developed in retirement. They had the experience of further education which would enable them to take up new studies with ease.* They had the professional status which would enhance their position in their communities and the secure self-image derived from years of creative achievement. They were able to taper off working hours gradually and take on part-time consultancy work in retirement if they wanted. And they had the means to enjoy these interests and resources free from material anxieties.

The car workers, on the other hand, had tended to make a complete break between work and life and had developed few skills or resources which could be carried over into retirement. (Trade union activity was one of the rare transferable skills.) Very few had had any further education since school and so lacked one incentive to make use of adult education. Work relationships began and ended at the factory gate, whereas the architects had on the whole made enduring friendships among colleagues. If work did have an influence on 'non-work' areas of life it was usually on the negative side. Shift work continued right up to the last day, making it hard for workers to join in activities within the community. Men working on the assembly line often

* Various sources, especially the General Household Survey, show that the extent of education experienced beyond childhood is strongly related to later participation in adult education.

found the job particularly tough in the last years at work and were often too tired to go out at the end of the day.

Assessments of adjustment to retirement are always rule-of-thumb, but it's worth recording that while 24 per cent of the architects reported problems in the early or later stages of retirement, the figure for the car workers was double this at 48 per cent.*

However well a particular job or profession prepares a man or woman for retirement there are still likely to be immense difficulties if the work *is* the life—difficulties expressed by the senior consultant quoted on page 126. Among those most vulnerable to this total identification with the working role are the self-employed. Mr F., a self-employed architect, had lived for his work for thirty-seven years. Then he was told he had to cut down his work load and finally to retire because of high blood pressure—this caused 'purely and simply' because of over-work. He describes his sense of shock: 'We spent several weeks in Cornwall. It was the longest holiday I'd ever allowed myself. But the time came when we had to come back . . . and it was only then that the change hit me. I mean others going to work . . . yourself left behind . . . as the months went by, gradually losing touch with all your old life, your old connections, the schemes you've dreamed of . . . and pride-wise becoming a nobody after being a somebody. My neighbour, Mr M. is the County Surveyor, he lives across the way there . . . I used to get up especially in the morning to see him going to the office. Talk about nostalgic . . . I used to eat my heart out to see him going off . . . and I sit at home, on the shelf.'

Mr F. admits to a miserable year followed by a slow-dawning appreciation of his regained health and new life. Two things particularly helped him: his good relationship with his wife who had always accepted his 'workaholism' and gave him much understanding help and those material resources which allowed him to plan trips abroad and take up golf with much of the enthusiasm he had devoted to architecture. Yet, still for Mr F.

* C. Phillipson, op. cit.

something has been lost; he has never recaptured the sense of direction he felt during his working life.

Mr F.'s retirement illustrates some important points. He has no 'good work' in his retirement which would allow him to transcend his own personal interests. He has also failed to find the kind of goals in retirement which would give his life meaning now that he is without the exigencies and deadlines of the work situation. For retirement is not just a question of replacing the old goals of work, but of finding appropriate new goals and developing new values. This is brought out in an illuminating American study by Margaret Clark.*

She interviewed eighty retired people aged sixty-plus: half of these were in a psychiatric hospital for the first time in their lives and half were living in the community and had suffered no mental or emotional problems in retirement. Margaret Clark found that the values of the two groups differed in remarkable ways. Both groups were searching for meaning in life; but while the hospitalized group were still driven to compete, the community group were attracted to an ethos of co-operation and a relaxed pursuit of wisdom. Both groups prized independence. However, the hospitalized group saw independence as a way of avoiding dependency on others whom they might have cause to mistrust; the community group, on the other hand, wanted to be independent in order to maintain their self-respect and preserve the freedom of other people. The hospitalized group saw self-development in terms of keen aspiration, progress and continued pursuit of former targets; the community group, instead, emphasized continuity and evolution. The ambitions and dreams of the hospitalized group kept them oriented towards an ever-diminishing future; time was the enemy. In contrast, the community group tended to live in the present; time was an old friend and what remained of it was to be cherished.

Margaret Clark comments that *while the hospitalized group had retained the values and goals characteristic of American culture generally, the community group had evolved an alternative way of life*. The need to

* M. Clark, 'Anthropology of Aging', *Gerontologist*, Vol. 7, No. 1., 1967.

evolve new values and goals at retirement, she writes, constitutes a 'social metamorphosis' which is just as demanding as the transition from childhood to adulthood. Obviously, you cannot build too much on one study, but there is the suggestion that in order to adapt to life in retirement you need to practise self-acceptance rather than self-advancement, co-operation rather than competition, concern rather than control of others, the mode of being rather than having. This agrees with Lily Pincus's 'recipe' for a good long life:* that underlying sense of your own value which is based on your capacity to value and care for others.

TWO RETIREMENTS

The retirement of Nicholas Evans and Norman H. are not typical of anyone but themselves. But they do illustrate some of the ideas about retirement I have been discussing.

1. Nicholas Evans Nicholas Evans grew up in a poor but close-knit family in the Welsh mining town of Aberdare. As a boy he had two passions, religion and art, both of which have continued to shape the pattern of his life. His family were devout Pentecostals and for Nicholas, too, the Pentecostal chapel became the centre of his life. While only in his teens he became a lay preacher, preaching on Sundays throughout the South Wales valleys. At school he liked painting best of all, even though the children were actively discouraged from individual creativity: 'I recall painting on a particular St David's Day. I was supposed to copy a dragon which was on the wall, but I did the claws my way and I also did the body of the dragon my way. Well, I remember the teacher chastising me because I hadn't made an exact copy. But I was doing it my way. I always knew I could paint.'

Nick was able to draw the way he pleased at the play centre which opened after school three times a week. He was given

* See page 96.

materials and encouragement by the supervisor, who took a particular kindly interest in the boy. But when the time came to leave school and go into the mines his art had to stop. Even so, he never completely lost the idea that one day he would paint and he consciously 'saw things in pictures', inwardly recording the harsh life of his fellow miners. These were the days of the Depression and the General Strike, of low-pay, grinding work, long hours, lock-outs and the fear of redundancy and dependence on the soup-kitchens. These sufferings Nick shared but he interpreted them in the light of his faith: 'I would say they were wonderful days for the children of God. They "felt the pinch" but they knew it helped form their character.'

Nick married and was to raise a family as close-knit as his parents. Still a young man, he left the mines for work on the railways where he stayed until his retirement. His life was his family, the church and the daily round at work—a round made no easier by the ill health which was the legacy of his years underground. As he got nearer retiring age, work became more of a struggle and both he and his wife looked forward with unreserved pleasure to the last day at work. 'When I retired from the railways I felt that the yoke had been broken, I felt free . . . I looked around for some months and then—the painting—what I had always wanted to do, what I knew I could do as a boy in school which had been suppressed for years and years, took my interest. But how was I to get at it? How was I to start? Then I remembered the time I was in the play centre . . .'

Nick began to draw in charcoal. There was never any doubt about his subject matter: his memories of the mines of the 1920s were as sharply delineated in his mind as if the intervening years had never been. His task was to find a way of translating that vision into paint and he soon evolved his own unmistakable style of drawing straight onto canvas and then modelling black and white paint with his fingers.

From the very first, he re-experienced all the excitement and curiosity he had felt about his art as a boy. He was overjoyed with the sense that at last he had come into his own: 'I was a sick man when I left the railways. Now I seem to have found a new lease of life, a new purpose of being, and behind it all is my religion. Would it surprise you if I say that I pray before I paint? That when I'm painting I'm praying? I give it to God as an offering, an act of worship, that's me, that's Nick Evans . . . I paint first for the glory of God. Then for the miner. When I paint I want to draw attention to how the miner suffered, how things were in the past so that we can improve conditions for all in the future . . . I am a miner's historian and don't want to paint anything else. There is a sense in which the past is with us now, so is the future here now.'

Nick Evans feels that his paintings come from the depths of his being, the source of his faith: he feels 'only a channel'. He admits to a near-obsession with his art. Yet however much he lives and dreams his pictures he does so in the middle of his family—not cut off from them—and with the encouragement of his neighbours and friends: 'When I have completed a painting I ask my friends to look at it. I watch their reactions. I ask my daughter, my sons—I need to watch their reactions, too, to know if I am progressing.'

He has become well known and his paintings are exhibited and hung in galleries. He says he is 'a happy man'.

2. Norman H. Norman H. is a stocky, nervously cheery man. He talks of his retirement from his job as a driving instructor with a mixture of self-dramatization and bewilderment—as though he was, in some sense, the passive victim of events which were outside his control; at the same time, there is no doubt about the suffering these events caused him: 'It was as if the structure of my life had collapsed—almost like being hit by a physical blow. I suddenly seemed to realize that I'd been working since I was sixteen, getting up, getting ready to go to work, going to work, coming back from work. It was a set habit—like breathing. And suddenly it finished. If it had been phased out I think it would have been very different. But it was a question of finishing the routine on a Friday, just like that. And then, after the first fine careless rapture, the feeling: God! What have I done?'

Norman H. was brought up in a Yorkshire wool town, the

second, late-born son of a comfortably-off business man and his wife, both of whom made no secret of the fact that Norman had been a 'mistake'. 'I still feel very bitter about my parents—even though I've always been a good son. I was told at a very early age I wasn't wanted. I've always been made to feel responsible for that. One of my parents' favourite expressions was: "You wouldn't be here if it wasn't for us"—as though they had done me a favour! I soon realized I was a nuisance to them: my mother used to say with such bitterness, "Children are no good to you."'

Norman's dream from boyhood had been to become a pilot, but he became shortsighted in his teens and he has never forgotten the disappointment he felt when the dream had to be set aside. At school he never felt that he was 'up to it' either in sports or studies. After leaving school early, he had a succession of jobs in business. He never stayed long because he always felt that the next job he contemplated would be the job that would make his future. One firm he joined in his late twenties went bankrupt and Norman was out of work and broke. He had a 'bad bout of depression' and then joined the merchant navy, feeling that he might perhaps begin to live the adventurous life he had always wanted. Then came the war and he stayed in the Navy, enjoying the happiest time of his life. He did well and was offered a commission. But he turned it down fearing the commitment that the new responsibilities would bring—and he now regrets this decision.

After the war, Norman married Mary, a Wren, came out of the navy and settled down in a small suburban commuter town in Hertfordshire. Mary had a job as a primary school teacher and Norman threw his energies into starting up a small engineering business. Both were busy with separate lives and put off indefinitely any ideas of having children. The marriage has lasted but it has never been a close one. Their only shared interest is holidaying abroad. Early on, Norman began a short-lived affair which was the first of a succession. Mary found out the first infidelity but, thereafter, chose to turn a blind eye and immerse herself in her work and circle of friends.

Norman's business never prospered. In the end, he sold up and took a job as a driving instructor where he stayed until his retirement. He never made any close friends among his colleagues and looked on his job as a necessary evil. His energies were kept for the string of hobbies he took up with unfailing enthusiasm and varying success. Two hobbies were most important: driving fast cars and sailing. He had very few acquaintances in his home town except for some drinking companions at the local pub, and some sailing enthusiasts at the boat club.

Norman looked forward to his retirement as a time of liberation. He and Mary would both have good occupational pensions. He spent much time planning the trips abroad they would make, the sailing he would do, the drum-playing lessons he would take. Four years before the earliest date he could leave work, he bought a little bungalow near his boat club. This caused friction at home because Mary had never properly been consulted and had no wish to spend much time away from their home town.

Norman persuaded Mary, who was ten years younger than himself, to retire with him so that they could spend much time in the first years of his retirement on longer trips abroad. Mary, who loved her job, agreed—but only reluctantly.

As soon as they retired, they set off on a Mediterranean cruise. Mary was withdrawn and depressed at the end of her teaching career. Norman had expected to feel on top of the world, but instead he just felt flat and slightly uneasy. He remembers a sinking feeling when a fellow passenger who asked about his retirement remarked: 'You should have gone on until you were sixty-five—you made a mistake.'

In the next few months Norman carried out the plans he had made, filling almost every minute of the day with his hobbies and his sailing. But he still felt oddly apprehensive and physically low. Meanwhile, Mary was slowly climbing out of her depression and beginning to look at openings in voluntary work.

One night Norman was alone at the bungalow and was seized with desperate feelings of panic and anxiety. He was so frightened by this attack that he went home to see his doctor, who prescribed tranquillizers; but they did not help the mounting depression he felt: 'I had a feeling as though pressure was building up inside me and something would go snap in my mind. I thought I was going insane and I wanted to die.'

He was obsessed with the thought that his life had been a failure: 'The trouble with retirement is you've got all this time to look back and see all the wrong decisions, all the things that went wrong in the horrible knowledge that you can't put them right *and there's no more time*.'

He no longer went out of the house, but his guilt about his past treatment of Mary made it impossible to share his feelings with her. In any case, one anxiety he could never have shared: the fear that he was being precipitated into old age and possible impotence, the realization that the casual affairs had had their day.

Norman H. gradually recovered: 'It was a bit like sailing in my dinghy, as if some unexpected force of wind had pushed me over and instead of going right under the boat slowly came back to an even keel.' He has reduced his earlier expectations of retirement, has lost the taste for foreign travel and plans his life round weekends in the bungalow and weekdays devoted to his latest hobby: pigeon-racing.

Conclusions It is only possible to understand these reactions to retirement by first understanding each man's individual life history and social environment at the point of retirement. Only then can we also see how each man's biography is also a response and reaction to influences of occupation, community and class. Nicholas Evans and Norman H. come from a deprived working-class and comfortable middle-class family background respectively. But one benefited from a secure and loving home while the other grew up with rejecting and censorious parents. Influenced no doubt by their childhoods, the two men showed quite different capacities to handle hardship and loss throughout life. Norman H.'s resistance to commit himself to job, wife and perhaps to children can also be interpreted as a defence against the pain of possible loss and failure.

Neither of the men were particularly well-educated, though Norman H. had the benefits of a grammar school as against Nick Evans's elementary schooling. Norman H.'s schooling had left him with enough confidence to take up new hobbies without any anxiety, but its overall effect had been to confirm his sense of inferiority. While Nick Evans's education had not prepared him in any way for further education he had learnt the rudiments of the art which was to shape his later years.

Both men were relatively well off materially at retirement. Nick Evans had benefited from an occupational pension and both Norman H. and Mary, his wife, enjoyed much larger ones. This meant that Nick Evans was free to follow his painting career and Norman H. to follow his more luxurious lifestyle. Clearly Norman H.'s financial security was not sufficient to ensure any happiness for him—although it may have had an important part in easing his return to 'normal' life after his breakdown.

Despite the harshness of Nick Evans's working career, there were always important continuities between his work and life which were absent from Norman H.'s career. One link was the faith which obliged him to bear the same witness at all hours of the day. He felt pride in his role as a worker and solidarity with his colleagues in the mines and, later, on the railways. At the back of his mind there was always the vague hope that one day he might express this solidarity in works of art. Many of his workmates lived in his community and those who retired with him would continue to be neighbours.

For Norman H. work and life had been compartmentalized. The job had had only a utilitarian value and had done little to boost his self-esteem. It had postponed but not prevented any need to face his inner conflicts and the instability in his marriage. Once, however, the anchoring effect of employment was removed the frailty of his identity was shown up in his subsequent collapse. This disintegration contrasts with the way Nick Evans was able to use his retirement to re-integrate aspects of his personality—his boyhood artistry, his faith, his experience as a worker—in his new role as a painter. In this he was supported by his good relationships with friends and family. Norman H., on the other hand, had no feeling of rootedness in his community and few outside friends. He and Mary had continued to have quite separate activities and social networks. There was much unspoken resentment and guilt between them and, at the point of retirement, a half-articulated clash of retirement goals when Mary reluctantly left her own job to step into the care-taking role that Norman H. expected of her.

These stories suggest that in retirement it is not activity alone that matters but the quality of activity: the extent to which it engages the whole person and can be perceived as useful. Despite the tight schedule of hobbies and sports Norman H. drew up, they did not allow him to transcend his own interests in any meaningful way: they were pastimes and brought no sense of self-fulfilment. But for Nick Evans, his painting was the realization of long-frustrated hopes and talents and was also the best way for him to serve God and man; in Schumacher's terms, it was 'good work'.

Norman H.'s difficulties in adapting to retirement can be linked to his failure to evolve appropriate values and goals. His attitude to life and activities was aggressive and competitive. He was dissatisfied with himself and his fate and constantly compared himself to others. He was oriented towards the bitterness of the past and the ever-diminishing future rather than to an enjoyment of the present. Nick Evans's adaptation to retirement must have been helped by his contemplative frame of mind and long-held personal and political commitment to co-operation rather than competition. His art both expressed and was made possible by his acceptance of his life history.

What is needed is far more understanding and help for those people who find the change from work to retirement a stressful and painful one.

There are important social measures which must be taken: flexible retirement, higher pensions, better social services. We need cheaper and more attractive education for the retired. We need more openings in community work. But these things will not be enough. Preparation for retirement should be widely available—but in a form which allows time for individual counselling and which lays emphasis on the continuing human need for 'good work'.

It is essential that this sketched programme should not be seen as another set of measures done *for* or *to* the retired. Older people themselves must be joint planners and agents. As Lily Pincus has pointed out, retired people today are better educated, less submissive and more articulate about their needs. They need to work together more closely within their own organizations, the unions and the political parties to influence the decisions that affect them. The struggle is both political and personal. It matters for all retired people if one individual carves out for himself a life in defiance of the stereotypes and social pressures. The Victorian rebel and writer, Edward Carpenter, put it much better. Replying to a congratulatory letter from friends on his seventieth birthday, he said: 'People should endeavour, more than they do, to express or liberate their own real and deep-rooted needs and feelings. Then, in doing so, they will probably liberate and aid the expression of the lives of thousands of others; and so will have the pleasure of helping, without the unpleasant sense of laying anyone under an obligation.'

Select bibliography

. . . Instead of listing all the many articles and books we have read while preparing this book, we have chosen to recommend these eleven, because we have found ourselves consulting them most often.

Lily Pincus and Aleda Erskine

Old Age, Simone de Beauvoir, Penguin Books, 1978. An extensive, if pessimistic, survey of attitudes to old age in past and present societies.

The View in Winter—Reflections on old age, Ronald Blythe, Allen Lane, Penguin Books, 1979. The author has listened to all kinds of people in and around their eighties and the book contains their candid views on old age and a considered, if sombre, interpretation by the author. Some fascinating material.

Why Survive: Being Old in America, Robert N. Butler, Harper and Row, New York 1975. A magisterial and deeply critical survey of all aspects of ageing.

An Ageing Population, Vida Carver and Penny Liddiard (Eds), Hodder and Stoughton in association with The Open University Press, 1978. A stimulating and useful collection of essays and extracts.

A Good Age, Alex Comfort, Mitchell Beazley, 1977. Brushing aside myths and stereotypes, the author, a leading authority, deals with various aspects of ageing with wit, vigour and directness.

Age and Vitality: Commonsense ways of adding life to your years, Dr Irene Gore, Unwin Paperbacks, 1979. A determined attack on the idea that growing old includes an inevitable severe mental and physical decline. Includes ways to improve vigour and vitality in later life.

Maggie Kuhn on Ageing—a dialogue edited by Dieter Hessel, The Westminster Press, USA 1977. The forthright views of the leader of the US Grey Panther movement in conversation with a fellow Christian.

The Emergence of Retirement, Chris Phillipson, Working Papers in Sociology No. 14, Department of Sociology and Social Administration, University of Durham, 1978. The author argues that ambiguities in the concept of retirement can be traced to the use of the elderly as a reserve labour force.

To the Good Long Life: What we know about growing old, Morton Puner, Macmillan, London 1978. A readable, well-researched and challenging exploration of the process of ageing and the 'new' generation of over-sixties.

The Measure of my Days, Florida Scott-Maxwell, Stuart and Watkins, London 1968. One woman's reflections on growing old: 'We who are old know that age is more than a disability. It is an intense and varied experience, almost beyond our capacity at times, but something to be carried high.'

Learning to Grow Old, Paul Tournier, SCM Press, London 1972. A Swiss doctor's philosophy of growing older. One of the few books to tackle this aspect of ageing.